Under the Spell

Under the Spell

A Novel

Benjamin Hedin

TriQuarterly Books / Northwestern University Press
Evanston, Illinois

TriQuarterly Books
Northwestern University Press
www.nupress.northwestern.edu

Printed in the United States of America

10 9 8 7 6 5 4 3 2 1

Library of Congress Cataloging-in-Publication Data

Names: Hedin, Benjamin, author.
Title: Under the spell : a novel / Benjamin Hedin.
Description: Evanston, Illinois : TriQuarterly Books/
Northwestern University Press, 2021
Identifiers: LCCN 2020052494 | ISBN 9780810143722
(paperback) | ISBN 9780810143739 (ebook)
Subjects: LCSH: Widows—Oregon—Fiction. |
Marriage—Fiction.
Classification: LCC PS3608.E3325 U53 2021 | DDC
813.6—dc23
LC record available at https://lccn.loc.gov/2020052494

Under the Spell

The fight with Lucrece began as soon as they got to the house. Because of a delay with the connecting flight the trip had taken almost ten hours, and when Sandra brought her bag to the guest room and asked if she wanted to lie down, Lucrece said no, I want to see my son's body.

"You what?"

She repeated the request. Sandra explained why that would not be possible, and Lucrece started to shout, you had no right, no right, and before she knew it Sandra was shouting too. Each accused the other of disgracing Dale's memory.

"You couldn't possibly know what he wanted," Lucrece said.

"It's not like this is something we ever discussed. I'll give you that."

Not one time, as far as she could remember. "Don't bury me in Indiana." He had said that once, but as a joke, while singing into his toothbrush. She had brought their mail into bed and was holding up a newsletter from some group named Friends of the Palmer Hotel.

"What is that?" she asked.

"One of the first supper clubs in the area. They're trying to bring it back. All the old-time crooners used to play there. Don't . . . don't . . . don't bury me in Indiana . . ."

"Is that an actual song?"

"No," he said, putting the toothbrush down. "Just my dying wish."

On the night he did die, the social worker gave her one form at a time, circling the relevant parts of each document. But Sandra was too dazed to think, and cremation seemed like the easiest choice. There was no casket or transportation to consider, and she wasn't sure, besides, if a mortician could present Dale's body for viewing. It never occurred to her if Lucrece would object or not.

"So how'd you leave it?" Cheryl asked the next morning.

"Compromised I guess."

"Compromised? How?"

"We'll still have a funeral. A formal one like Dale's father had, with the robes and candles and chanting. I didn't think you could you know."

"Could what."

"Don't you need a body for a funeral?"

"It's only hard-core Catholics who believe that."

"You're telling me Dale's family is not hard-core?"

"Sweetheart," said Cheryl, "you ain't seen nothing yet. And that's not chanting, by the way. It's singing."

"Sounds like chanting," Sandra said. "Like spoken word or Sanskrit meditation. We have a club near campus that does it. First Tuesday of every month."

The dream that night was different. She knew he would be there, summoned instantly, as if with the click of a lighter. Sleep was their meeting ground, but in her dreams there were always two of her, the one acting out whatever was going on and another who knew it to be a fiction, who was there to say no, you are not at the table together, he is gone. Or, you think this is real, but it is only a sign you are sleeping.

Tonight, though, something else happens. She cannot recall the events of the dream. Some peculiar contrivance of memory. She is in a theater, giving notes, Dale enters to say the restaurant has no more tables, they will have to get carryout, something like that. But it is enough for her to be tricked, for that other self to disappear, and when she wakes, two hours or two minutes later—she is not sure which—she realizes that in the dream she had forgotten he was dead. Even now it was like he was still here. She was in his slipstream.

At the funeral, though it was the service for her own husband, she felt like an outsider, an anthropologist conducting fieldwork, documenting some ritual. She looked at the design on the priest's robe and counted the candles on the altar, wondering why some were lighted and others were not. During the receiving line she studied one of the figures carved into the stained glass, the portrait of a man in a suit coat and pince-nez. The priest told her he had been the church's reverend during the storm of 1962 and raised the collection money necessary to have the window replaced after it was knocked out.

"So did he put himself up there?" Sandra asked. "Or did others?"

"Others I think."

The priest motioned at some people waiting to shake hands.

"You guys always seemed like the perfect couple to me."

"You'll have children yet. Watch. You've got your whole life in front of you."

"And to think, for this to happen at New Year's. Of all times."

But there was always something to read into the calendar, she reflected. Always symbolism in the offing. Dale's death would have been just as meaningful, just as tragic, at the start of spring or fall or in the middle of summer, really any date you choose.

Then again, this man—Buxter was his name, and he also taught at Clatsop—did not mean what he said. No one did. These words she was hearing, the promises and offers of consolation, were not words in the ordinary, conventional sense. They were part of the performance, like the Latin text and priest's vestment, showing our need to do something, anything, in the face of the enormity of death. Like pipers beating in the surf, Sandra thought, the sensory bells going off in their brains, not knowing which way to run.

The reception was at Lighting Works, the brewery owned by Cheryl's husband, Wayne. The staff brought around steins printed with Lighting Works' logo, an *L* and *W* made with three axes, meant to evoke Oregon's timber culture. Sandra sat at a table in the corner, watching the lights flicker up and down the brewing kettles, and listened to the toasts, the stories that were told about Dale.

Like when he wouldn't let someone cut in line at the Holland Tunnel, rolling down his window and muttering, "Qué? Qué? No hablo inglés."

Or how he hired a chef for his bachelor party to make breakfast for everyone. That decision was money, said someone who had been there. Money.

And all of it was true, at least in the sense that these incidents had happened, but in the telling Sandra noticed something else at work. Whoever was talking about Dale felt the need to make him funnier, or saintlier, than he had actually been. They seized on details, lines of dialogue, that were unimportant but now seemed prophetic, revealing.

Death is the best career move. That was a saying she knew, though not the source. Some TV personality or cynic, she seemed to remember.

A man came up and placed a business card in front of her.

Best Day Clinic, it said, underneath the address and a caption: Helping You Get There.

"My wife," he said, "Jenny Travers. She's one of the doctors who volunteers at this place. Three days a week."

When her phone rang she was grateful for the interruption, though she recognized the number as the district attorney's. He wanted to know if he could access Dale's medical records. They were moving ahead with a charge of manslaughter.

"I thought you already had those."

"No. Just the accident report."

What for, she wanted to ask, but it wasn't hard to conjure some reason. To show Dale's death was not due to a preexisting condition—that he had not expired from a heart attack, say—or some other loophole a defense attorney might try and open up.

"Yes," she said. "Go ahead. You have my permission."

Anderson was the last to leave, as she knew he would be. They were in the parking lot. Cheryl, who was driving, was about to pull the car around. Anderson was fiddling with his tie, starting to unknot it but then hesitating, as if even though the memorial had ended it would still be some sort of solecism to ditch his formal wear.

She wanted to say, there's nothing I can do, nothing I can give you that won't make you feel this way. At last she did say it.

"You know that, don't you?"

"Yes," he answered.

"Do you know how I know?"

"Because you feel it too."

"Right. I could have talked him out of it. Or gone with—or called after him. Or this and this. Anything would have been enough. One second would have been enough."

And suddenly she was upset with him for lingering like this, seeking absolution or not even, simply clarity, trying to determine what his role was in the order of things.

But this was not something she had the power to grant.

Lucrece suggested they inventory his belongings and make two piles, to keep and give away. Sandra went along with it, though everything Lucrece boxed she was going to unpack again later. "I'll take only what fits in my suitcase," Lucrece boasted, claiming the tassel from his mortarboard and the sweater he had worn on the day he came home from college. Sandra knew if she said everything stays, I'm not ready, she would open herself up to charges of wallowing, of indulging in self-pity and sentiment. "His things are not what counts," Lucrece had said, and Sandra had wanted to reply, "But they do. They count very much."

"Um, excuse me?" Lucrece said, holding up a pair of snow pants. They were two or three sizes too big, the knees patched with duct tape. "Story please."

"We flew to Vail one time," Sandra said, "and the airline lost our luggage. He didn't want to buy new ones, and this place we rented skis from, it's all they had. Lost and found."

"And they fit him?"

"Well he had to wear like four pairs of long johns, plus workout pants."

"Giveaway obviously."

"Sure."

But even these she wanted to hold onto, not just the pants but the lift ticket hanging from the belt clip. It had the day on it, the day and the year.

"He loved that about you, that you would fly off somewhere at the last minute."

No, Sandra almost said, you misunderstood. It wasn't the last minute. But then she let it go. This was as close as Lucrece would get to an apology, an act of truce.

In his study they found things she couldn't explain, whose provenance was uncertain. An anklet, the multicolored beads chipped, a relic from summer camp, she guessed, though she was at a loss to say why he had kept it. Notes on stationery written in some galactic code. *PS*14 > 32*x*. And a tintype, the sepia washed out along the edges, the image of an arroyo with shells glinting along its bank.

"Where is that?" Lucrece asked.

"I have no idea."

"It's beautiful."

Sandra put the tintype on her nightstand. And the ankle bracelet. It would come to her one of these days, where they were from, though there was no rush to remember. It was something to wait for.

Her engagement ring she put in a baize-lined case. Something her mother had given her, a relic from the days of steamships, with the insignia of one, the *Wellington*, branded on its laminate top. Meant for cigars or poker chips, she could not remember which. The wedding band she was unsure about. Widows wore it on the right hand—she had heard that once. Was it true? She tried it out, switching hands, opening more of the packages that had arrived that week. Boxes of tea and chocolate, lilies, peonies, and lilacs. Bottles of wine clustered on the counter like bowling pins.

The ashes she did not know what to do with. Lucrece had wanted to bury them in Indiana. Absolutely not, Sandra said, though she knew Lucrece was entitled to a portion of them. She drove to the mortuary and described the situation, saying she was not ready to open the urn. "Certainly," said the owner, but he forgot to close the door all the way, and through the hinges Sandra saw him lift the top and undo the knot of cellophane. He used a small, pointed scoop, the powder dry and airy.

At the airport she gave Lucrece the tin.

"No," she said, and told Sandra she had paid for a nameplate to go in the church where the funeral was held, in the memorial chapel beside the altar.

"Put the ashes there."

A call at the church confirmed the order, and the man on the phone, the priest or whoever, told her since no one would be at the parsonage that afternoon she was free to leave the ashes in the mail slot.

She did that, writing "Tobin, D" on a Post-it and tying it to the tin with a rubber band.

Her parents left the next day. They checked out of the hotel, intending to use the guest room now that Lucrece was gone, but at dinner she said, "Maybe you guys should think about looking at flights."

They protested, said their plan was to stay on indefinitely, for as long as she needed them. No, she said. Too much going on. Too much to think about. There was the affidavit for the prosecutor, documents for the probate attorney.

"Go home and wait for me," she said.

And it was true, in part. The mechanics of dying: nobody talks about those. All the chores and bookkeeping that come from being the one left behind.

But really she wanted to be alone with him. That's what it was. His mug was on the drying rack, his shirts in the dryer. She wanted everyone out of the house so she could take stock, figure out how to say goodbye to him.

"Don't be too long," her mother told her, and she almost said, what is long, what is short, for she felt as though she had been liberated from time, relieved of its burden. Check all the timetables, she thought, all the schedules. Tell me which one has your spouse dying at thirty-five on it.

She searched for estate lawyers after receiving the credit card statement for December. She hung up on two after an automated prompt put her on hold. Richard Rawlings, the next number she tried, answered the phone himself. She began by saying, "Thank you for taking my call," which sounded odd, she thought, since she was the one hiring him.

"Can I ask you some things?"

"Shoot."

"His credit card debt—what happens to that?"

"I'll take a look at it. Some of it's forgiven. These are personal charges, right?"

From next door came the sound of a crank being turned. Her neighbors were reeling their awning in. She watched the squall blow down the river and mist over the lights of the tankers moored in the harbor. A canopy of shadow settled over the drive, and rain was pelting her windows and gutters.

"Yes, but he had a business too," she said. "Vestiture. An LLC. And a nonprofit that he teamed with, and made videos for. Not for any real money though."

"What was their name?"

"Higher Plane. Listen, I'm sorry, I know you get this a lot, but I have no money. What's it based on, a percentage of what you save?"

"My fee? It's determined by how much work goes into the estate, the size of the assets and so on."

"Fair enough."

"So you mentioned the fiscal sponsorship. How about the family? Anything large, any properties, annuities, or co-ownerships?"

"No. Nothing like that. He had some stock. Shares from his last contract with BAE. British Airways. He was a research analyst for them."

"Okay. So let's get started and settle my fee later. Though there is the matter of you."

"Of me."

"You don't want this happening to you."

"You are referring to dying."

"Dying intestate. Do you have a will? It doesn't take long to set one up."

"I'll think about it," Sandra said. "Maybe next time."

The dean canceled her class, Introduction to Directing. Summarily too, without any consultation from her, and she wondered if a male instructor would be treated the same, or given a choice of whether to teach or not. The students had already been notified, he said, adding that of course she would get paid for the term.

That was the important thing, she nearly said. Because it was true, she had almost no money. That wasn't just a line she told Richard Rawlings. Even if she borrowed against her IRA, she would have to find another job, and if it was an academic appointment that started in the fall, then the savings would probably run out before then. She would have to redeem the shares or sell the house. She asked Cheryl for the name of a realtor, and she came back with Beth Markson of Beth Markson Properties. Sandra called to schedule a tour.

"This place is beautiful," Beth said as they were standing in the kitchen.

"Wait till you see upstairs. None of it is finished."

"It doesn't matter. A Bradstreet is a Bradstreet."

"A what is a what?"

"The architect of this house. You can't price that, having his name on it. And don't worry about the repairs. The listing writes itself. Beautiful historic property looking for TLC. And we'll see what we can do before then."

A contractor was on his way, was what she meant by that. Sandra watched him pull up in a van with the windows painted over, the word "Insured" lettered on the side. He knelt in front of the porch and shined a flashlight over the pilings, and she winced while they toured the upstairs, believing the house's condition gave the wrong impression of Dale, that he was a loafer or dilettante. Tufts of carpet were poking out from the trim. The floor was mottled, with scuff marks like clouds on a watch crystal. Beth rolled a racquetball to identify the spots where the boards were warped. There used to be three rooms up here, Sandra explained, one wall knocked down to make a sculpture gallery. She pointed to the trace of the old crown moldings.

"How bad is it?" she asked after they had toured each floor.

"All in?" said the contractor. His coat was labeled Steven, but he had introduced himself as Bill. "Hard to say. Eighty, ninety. Maybe more."

He showed her the list. His handwriting was messy, but some of the words stood out. Sumps. LR pipes. Patio door. Backsplash. Walls.

"Remember," said Beth, "it's not your money. We'll wrap it into the purchase price."

"But somebody's got to pay for it now," she said. "The whole reason I'm doing this is because I don't have any money. So let's sell it as is."

"You'd be giving up a lot," Beth said. "I think it's better to wait."

"No," said Sandra. "No, definitely not."

There was a card in the drone, from his last shoot, a film on coastal erosion commissioned by the Environmental Protection Agency. He had texted her to say the police drove up and thought his permits were counterfeit. So think about contacting the nearest bondsman. And ten minutes later: okay I talked them out of it but that was scary. She backed the footage up to a hard drive and pressed play over a random spot. He was testing the wind, hovering at a range of altitudes before dropping down to the shore and up the path of an estuary, chasing an egret from the shallows, the tube of its neck coiled between the tall reeded bones of its wingspan. As he piloted the drone around she saw him, a mistake no doubt, or still part of the test, but there he was, on the beach in his jeans and sand-colored boots, consulting the monitor, the wind touching his hair, lifting that dapple of blond at his temples.

She asked Richard Rawlings if he would contact the EPA.

"I mean, I could do it," she said, "but so could you. You are my lawyer."

"Right. It's more formal if I do it. How much payment have they sent?"

"What?"

"Did they pay him anything up front, or was it on delivery?"

"I have no idea."

"Right. So please send me that contract and everything else."

She forwarded him their bank statements and credit card bills, and was going to do the same for Vestiture, only to discover she did not know any of Dale's passwords. Brooklyn10, the one they used for their retirement account, did not work for his email or the bank account he used for business. She went back to his email and clicked on "Forgot password?" and was taken to a set of security questions.

In what city were you born?

Easy. French Lick.

What was the name of your first dog?

Max, she typed, but the answer was rejected. She tried again. A new set of questions appeared on the screen.

Max. That was the name of the Norwegian elkhound Lucrece bought when Dale was five. She was sure of it. Did he have a dog before then?

What is your favorite food?

Spaghetti, but that was wrong too, and she closed the browser and reopened it and tried again. The questions now were even stranger. What is the model of car you would most like to own?

There was nothing she could do. An access code could be sent to Dale's phone, but his phone was at the bottom of the Columbia River. Then she remembered the tablet. It was new, he had bought it at a Black Friday sale, and she found it on a shelf in the living room, above a stack of Christmas cards. When she opened the browser his inbox came up, and she immediately changed the password to Brooklyn10. He had received forty-five messages since New Year's, mostly mass solicitations—Today We Are Asking for Your Help, Limited Time Free Shipping on All Orders—but there were also notes from his colorist and the agent he bought insurance from.

I'm sorry, I will not require workers' comp this year—I'm dead.

That would make a good opening line, she thought. You could write a play or novel with that beginning. The main character a ghost who wants to set everything to right, to atone for his misdeeds, but he can't—he's a ghost. A parable about the futility of remorse, about not waiting until the last minute.

No doubt, though, this sort of thing had been done already, and she wasn't dreaming up the premise, but recalling something she had read, years ago, and forgotten.

Mornings she marveled at the silence of the house. Hours before dawn, she would sit in the breakfast nook of the kitchen, waiting for the first rosy palings to appear, the streaks of lavender cracking through the dome of the sky. She had not known quiet like this, she figured, since she was six or seven and learning to dive in the neighborhood pool. Swimming farther down, to see if she could touch the bottom of the deep end.

The class secretary emailed to say he was placing a notice in the alumni magazine, wondering if she would like to contribute.

"Did you two meet in the old Tutwiler survey? I just want to make sure I have the details right. Sounds like an amazing story."

How he had heard of the accident she did not know. Sandra had not posted anything to Facebook or Twitter, and the story in the *Daily Astorian* was just a sidebar. COLLISION CLAIMS LIFE OF LOCAL CAMERAMAN. In truth Dale's death had been forgotten almost at once. New Year's deaths are remembered only in the aggregate, and it had not been an exceptional year. Fourteen fatalities in the state of Oregon, she had read, a number that was not up or down, simply the mean.

She began composing a reply. The class secretary had not specified if it was to be a tribute or an obituary. Was there a difference?

Dale and I met in Tutwiler's famous God in the World seminar, it's true. Though actually we had met before. Our halls did a mixer during freshman orientation. What's funny is that Reed Kovics, Dale's best friend, remembered it, and I didn't, and Dale didn't. So we met at the beginning and we met at the end. Those were the botched attempts. For five years after college we did not see each other, until we met in New York, at the party of another Class of '05 graduate. This time was for keeps, though Dale told me he was moving to Oregon. Pledged to a famous cinematographer, Mel Tomasinsky. That sounds like a made-up name, I said. And it was: Mel escaped from wartime Europe using borrowed papers, and kept the name ever afterward. In part because he did not want anyone to know what happened to his family. They were all gassed, and he said to Dale once that was his business and no one else's.

But it was true, Dale was going to be the executor of his estate and archives. It was only supposed to last for six months, and he asked if I wanted to come with. I thought he was joking, but that's how we ended up here, in an old house where restoration had started and then stopped, the owner leaving on the fly.

Dale very much treasured his four years at the school, all the more so as we got older. You might like to know he shot campus before he died, a panorama of the lawn to give to some friends who were getting married there. That image can be viewed here:

She scrolled up to proofread it and add they were the only seniors in God in the World, had put off fulfilling the same general education requirement. But the piece was already too long, and what had she said? Nothing important, nothing that admitted what was essential or enduring about their marriage. Just the things anyone would say.

"Want to come with?"

He had said it twice, and the first time she could not tell if he was serious or not. Since the party in Brooklyn he had not uttered one word about Oregon or Mel Tomasinsky or Mel Tomasinsky's niece, who lived in the same building as Dale and had arranged their meeting.

"What about your other job?" she asked, though she barely knew what that was. Research analyst was his title, but he seemed to travel a lot, testing cameras and drones, and in their conversation referred to these trips as being "on location."

Still, it didn't matter if he was joking. She had to say no, lest she seem too desperate, too eager to move things along with her new boyfriend.

But she couldn't do it, couldn't turn down the chance to spend four days with him. She said yes.

They flew to Seattle, their seats on opposite ends of the plane since she bought her ticket at the last minute, and drove the Pacific Coast Highway to Astoria. Five hours in the car, with stops in the old fishing towns, and the shared hotel room at the end. And the whole time she was thinking, I have found my double. It was astonishing how alike they were. Graduates of the same college, with the same aspirations and points of orientation, not having to explain who Fellini was, or Big Brother and the Holding Company. If couples spend so much time acquiring their own language, a set of reliable affinities, they had skipped that stage. They were already there.

Marriage, when it came, was different. She taught theater and filmmaking while knowing she would never direct another film again, took foundational courses in biology—as a faculty member at Clatsop, they were free—and moved on to her doctorate, a dissertation on marine ichnology. It was Dale who turned to filmmaking. When Mel died of an embolism, three months after they moved to Astoria, he decided to split his time between handling the estate and freelancing as a DP.

They were not doubles, then, not now, ten years on. Yet both were comfortable in their work, in the essential solitariness of it, and didn't seem to need the things everyone else did. The house, for instance. Though their friends regarded it as strange, even a little subversive, four years after closing they had still not finished any repairs or shown a willingness to clean up the wreckage they inherited.

So they had drifted apart, the way planetary bodies will whose orbits had shifted, only to discover larger, more structural similarities. The kind you see when zooming away from the surface.

That was what the class secretary needed to know.

"I'm going to have to write you back," she typed in response to his query, deleting everything else she had written. "I'll tell you all about it."

Reed, who had been unable to make the memorial service, offered to fly out, and she agreed, though she did not particularly want company. She had to clean the guest room. There had been no time for that when Lucrece was here, and she had forgotten to, anyway. Sandra had done most of her writing in this room, at a rolltop desk bought at one of the antique shops downtown, its lid slatted like an accordion, the initials of a previous owner carved into one corner. When she opened the top, she saw a draft of her dissertation, books stuck into other books to mark a page. Blue slips, interlibrary loan requests, and the close-up of a fossil, the valve of an ancient mussel, russet colored and notched on one side, as if it had been shaped with a file, marked like a sacred stone.

She stacked these in the fireplace and changed the linens, finding one of Lucrece's socks in the sheets. In the closet were things Dale had saved from Mel's estate sale, invoices and a stack of reel canisters with masking tape peeling from the rims, the film inside glossy and saw-toothed. An antique viewfinder hung from the doorknob, and there was a photo of Mel on a crane, cantilevered out over a glade of ferns and a lagoon in which you could see the reflection of the soundstage.

She called the curator of the film museum to let her know she was coming down with a drop-off. She drove to Goodwill first, and lifting the box Lucrece had packed, began to feel dizzy. Her heart wouldn't let her breathe, it was pumping so hard, and her hearing had shut off in one ear. She leaned on the window until she could get back in the driver's seat. The next thing she knew a voice said, "Traffic on the loop," and a blast of wind shook the car. She could not remember turning the radio on, and in the mirror above the visor she saw her face was creased, dented from the grip of the wheel.

The next day it happened again. When she went into the basement to take pictures for Beth everything started to heave, the windows and their locks, a pipe socket, the console of the water heater in front of her. Like none of it was fastened down, her vision collapsing into two binocular holes. She sat on the lowermost stair and counted to ten and then to twenty until the dizziness had passed.

She typed "grief vertigo" in a search engine and fell into a sinkhole of pages about mourning, reading heat scans of the brain and ads for antianxiety drugs, charts showing suicide rates for the bereaved. Customs written during the Victorian age, dos and don'ts. No chilled foods, for instance, not for those suffering from irreparable loss.

Last month on NPR there was an interview with a doctor named Comstock, who had written a book called *Under the Spell: Journeys into Grief*. In it he profiled survivors of every imaginable catastrophe, widows of mob hits, those who had fled a tsunami, parents who lost their child in a school shooting. And in the aftermath, he said, anything was possible. It was beyond the power of medicine or pharmacology to predict. People might forget their names or sue for divorce, become hunger artists, fasting for a year, or wander the hallway of their high school and break down in front of their old locker. Rob banks, perform unaccountable acts of charity. One man whose wife died in a helicopter accident adopted the son of the pilot. Clairvoyance had been reported, moments of glimpsing the unseen. "Like getting to the top of a mountain," Comstock said, "and looking out over the clouds."

Why no, Sandra thought. Put it like that and it almost sounds romantic, a state you would want to be in. It's not that way at all.

She was picking at a plate of food when Richard Rawlings called. All she could eat these days were dishes that when they emerged from the microwave were cold in the center and boiling on the edges, the skin of broccoli smeared across the wrapper.

"Dale's BAE shares," he said. "Were they the only ones he had?"

"I think so. Why?"

"They're gone."

"They're what?"

"They were in your account this time last year. Then he moved them to Vestiture, and in July they disappeared. Wiped from the statement. What happened in July?"

"I have no idea."

"Do you think he sold them?"

"No."

"Can you get them to me?"

"Not if they're gone."

"The certificate numbers, I mean."

"What penalties are we talking about? The IRS."

"Don't worry about that."

"But worst case?"

"Worst case? Well I can think of plenty. But let's hold off on that. Just send anything that has to do with BAE. It doesn't matter how old it is."

July. She could not remember him mentioning a sale. They were both worried about money, yet those shares, he always said, were a fail-safe, a thing to fall back on.

As in now. For times like these.

She opened his email and found nothing about a stock sale, only a donation, a letter from a nonprofit, and a note from an accountant Sandra had never heard of with IRS form 8283 attached. She sent these to Richard Rawlings.

When she turned back to the inbox a new message had come in.

Hey, hope you had a nice New Year's. Mexico was amazing. Wish I had photos to share—Carol said we should take some to prove we left the beach for more than five minutes but we didn't. So there you go.

And no sign of Paco. I looked.

Back to reality. Editing, mostly. Send me some news when you can.

The name of the person who sent this was Ryan Whitehurst. Sandra did not know him, or did not think she did. One of Dale's fraternity buddies, no doubt, or a colleague from BAE. Not among the recipients of the note she sent on the day Lucrece arrived. "Hello, and I know some of you know this already, but Dale died on New Year's."

She clicked to read the rest of the conversation history.

Hey, sorry again. During the week I work ALL THE TIME. Also I presently feel like my head has been hit with an anvil.

No, I can't make any promises! I had oral surgery yesterday and I'm not even sure I can make it to 9.

Let's just say 9 then. I won't be too far away—in Studio City.

I'm tied up until 9 and pretty bad company after—twelve hours of staring at the Avid leaves me brain dead. Is tonight yr only free evening?

What time are we looking at tomorrow, 8 or thereabouts?

I wish I could but we're on a tight deadline getting in the master archival this week and I got to log that and prep and get the EDL running. But I'd love to see you after, if yr free?

Tuesday I'll be running around pretty much all day picking up lenses and doing a few location scouts, but probably free by seven or so. Do you want to have dinner then?

Sounds like fun. Yes, I will be here. Let me know when yr free!

Hey, so those dates are locked for that Bruisemaker thing I told you about. I'll be in town 16–19, Tuesday through Friday. Let me know if you're around.

Ryan Whitehurst. In his signature Atlas Productions was the name of the company he worked for, the address on Los Feliz Boulevard in Los Angeles. According to their website they produced animated shorts and documentaries—one of them had won an Emmy—and under the commercials tab she found Dale's project, an advertisement for a sports car. He had been one of three DPs on the shoot, in charge of the drone, panning high above a hill in Mexico where a coupe darted up and down a series of switchbacks.

When she searched for the name Ryan Whitehurst four threads came up. The first was titled "Accounts."

It's nice to meet and I'm really looking forward to working on this. Stan gave me the gist over the phone but can you send the formal list of specs when you have a chance? Thanks so much.

So it was another job outstanding. But what? The music video featuring the band Bruisemaker had debuted the week before Christmas. As far as she knew, the EPA was the only gig Dale was working on.

She opened one of the other threads. This one had no subject line.

We're going to drive down for the road trip, it's like twenty hours but that's the point, the girl girl Thelma Louise thing and then fly back. Everyone said it's crazy to stack a vacation week on top of the holidays but I said it's crazy to ask someone to jump in full tilt on January 2. You'll back me on that, right?

She scrolled, not even bothering to read Dale's half of the correspondence, focusing only on the notes by Ryan Whitehurst.

> It's insane. None of the people know who you are but they are applauding as you walk down the photo line. There are three poses, three banks of photographers, and you don't even know who to look at or where to smile. You just keep doing it and pretend you know what you're doing. Like you've been there before.

> Yes, excellent to see you as well though I was pretty hungover and getting through the day was a challenge. I managed to sit in the convention hall for our presentation but skipped out on the rest. Thought I'd go see some of the town. Whatever there was to see.

> That screening's at LPR, right? There's a bar about a block from there called the Dove that's not bad. It's a cocktail-y place, but it's quiet, which is sort of the only thing I'm after in a bar these days. I could meet you there whenever? Or let me know if you had another spot in mind!

She turned to some of Dale's emails.

> Shooting in Whistler, not the resort but one of the mountains behind, following this band of snowboarders who I guess are also a cult. They're Bolivian, trace their roots back to some tribe there. Tacking on a few days at the end, a friend is flying out. It's a good opportunity. The producers are tight with the programmers at Sundance—I think you saw their last film, on bicycle messengers? You were the one to turn me onto it.

> That's the thing about travel, is the comedown. Reentry. Last session yesterday I was already sleepwalking. And then hurting on the trip home. Honestly the plane could have gone down and I wouldn't have noticed.

Stop, she told herself. Hold on. Back away.

The notes were a scam. They had to be. She was being baited by one of those pranksters who stalk the internet, reading obituaries and conviction notices with just this sort of ruse in mind.

Comstock, in the interview he gave for *Under the Spell*, had mentioned how the bereaved are easy targets for predatory lending. She should have never opened the emails. Simply by doing that she may have compromised her files and passwords.

Try as she might, however, she could not do it, could not convince herself it was a con. Whoever was doing it would have to write both sides of the correspondence, and the notes were too accurate and detailed, and what was the payoff? Not a request for money or nude photos. Send me some news when you can. That was all.

On the Atlas website Ryan Whitehurst was listed as associate producer on several projects. There was no picture. She tried LinkedIn, found too many returns, and Google images gave back nothing but pictures of men. A marine portrait, a runner in a BYU singlet, carrying a baton.

Twitter was set to private; she could not tell if it was the same Ryan Whitehurst, but among the Facebook accounts was a bio that read Atlas Productions. Sandra scrolled through the profile pictures: Ryan Whitehurst in a kayak, in the desert beside an antique gas pump, posing on the red carpet in a Stetson. In another she stood near a trellis with Christmas lights, holding a clutch that from the designer's initials on the clasp Sandra recognized as one she had owned herself, a few years ago. She had a faint overlay of freckles, and a pout, a biting glance of insouciance, that was her default expression. She couldn't be older than twenty-eight, and none of the photos featured a boyfriend. According to the profile she had graduated from USC. A film studies major, no doubt, with some connection to the industry, a father or uncle who worked at one of the studios.

Sandra got up and opened the window. Rain was licking through the screen. A garbage tub being wheeled to the curb. She clicked on the earliest emails—what she had to do was establish a chronology—but her wrists were fluttering. Surely by now she would be all grieved out. Or should be. No sleep, the adrenaline drained away, what was left for her body, her defenses, to summon? Yet she could barely keep track of the cursor.

Nine months after the car commercial wrapped Ryan Whitehurst wrote to say they were using some of the B-roll they had shot that day in a documentary. For three months nothing, then Atlas hosted a party during the American Film Market in October. They started writing not long after.

> Yeah, it's a hard thing for people to understand. There's no such thing as final or best. It's why Apple got rid of USB ports. Obsolescence is built in.
>
> Hey, did you get tickets for the opening night film? It says no passes left?

> I did actually. Had to do it—it's her first film in what, ten years? And I want to see the Q-and-A after. I'm not sure if she's really yr thing (it's all a little too obtuse and meandering for me, to be totally honest) but I think she's kinda fascinating and strange, so that should at least be interesting? I dunno.

Ryan Whitehurst liked abbreviation. She wrote "yr" for "your" and "omg" and "tbd" and a host of other sayings Sandra found annoying.

No, I do like her, Dale had written back,

> I just think she gets away with stuff that would never be allowed. Left turns an up-and-comer would be slayed for, you know? But good for her. Seriously. You get to a certain point where you have carte blanche.
>
> Let me know when you get in. That afternoon I'm going to the shorts program.

Most of the notes were like that, short and sent sporadically, increasing in frequency the closer they got to a film festival or one of his California trips. Clearly there was some tacit agreement that candor or intimacy was not to be allowed, or not indulged in for any great length. Dale had told her about the hip replacement surgery Lucrece had needed. Ryan Whitehurst replied:

> I know, you regard yr parents' age with a funny kind of ambivalence—grateful for what you have but also, well, it's just a little too much to hold in mind. I sort of go limp thinking about it. My dad is recovering from back surgery. It's hard to see him so irritated by his compromised mobility, and to know that it's only gonna get harder.

Otherwise it was all industry gossip and shop talk, and so what? Sandra thought, pouring herself a glass of wine. Set aside the initial panic, and what had she found? A casual, aimless flirtation, an idle correspondence. Not the sort of thing one could realistically expect a marriage to exclude.

She read the notes again with this interpretation in mind, but now discovered things she had missed the first time around. There was no mention of herself, for instance. A single reference, at the very beginning, after Dale had attended the Atlas party at the American Film Market.

> My wife, she won the audience award at SXSW for her first film, then decided it wasn't what she wanted anymore. She studies marine paleontology now.

That was it. Never any mention of "she" or "my wife" or "us." It was "I" in every note.

And there was something else, something, in the days ahead, she would conclude was even worse. Ryan Whitehurst knew things about Dale that no one except Sandra knew.

> The traffic last night, east-west, oh my God you would have died. It would have broken you. I ended up sleeping on Cassandra's couch because it would have been two before I got home.

Traffic. Dale could not stand traffic, or driving at all, really, and would mutter constantly at other drivers. For his birthday one year Sandra had a set of bumper stickers made with his favorite sayings, "The accelerator, it's the one on the right" and "Why are you in the left lane, do you just like the view better?" and he stuck them all over his Prius.

Other intimacies she had penetrated: describing a party the week of the Emmys, where the only other women in the room were serving drinks, and none of the nominated producers seemed eager to talk to her. "Ghosted," was what she had written. "Completely invisible. But you know. It's a long way to the top if you want to rock and roll."

AC/DC. Dale was very careful about keeping his AC/DC obsession under wraps. When they drove to Portland to watch a tribute band perform one of AC/DC's 1981 concerts note for note he swore her to secrecy.

"I don't think there's a need for that, love," Sandra had said.

"You think it's okay as a guilty pleasure."

"As just a regular plain old pleasure."

It could be a coincidence, but she didn't think so. "It's a Long Way to the Top" was not one of their better-known songs.

The last time they saw each other was in July, at a film festival in Carmel. Then LA, two months ago, when Ryan Whitehurst put off seeing him. It was her idea to meet—I'd love to see you after, if yr free—but she backed out of it:

> I'm tied up until 9 and pretty bad company after—twelve hours of staring at the Avid leaves me brain dead. Is tonight yr only free evening?

> Let's just say 9 then. I'll be up there and close to Studio City.

> I can't make any promises! I had oral surgery yesterday and I'm not even sure I can make it to 9.

She's really laying it on, Sandra thought. Throwing the kitchen sink at him. Maybe that was why Dale had not written back, whereas the guilt of lying made her reach out again after midnight.

> I'm sorry! During the week I work ALL THE TIME. Also I presently feel like my head has been hit with an anvil.

At 12:04: that was when she sent it. And not written again until today.

> Back to reality. Editing, mostly. Send me some news when you can.

It sounded straightforward and innocent—all of the emails did, that was the point, to deny any depth, any superstructure of meaning—but Sandra could guess its hidden intention. Ryan Whitehurst did not want him to think she was cutting off all contact. Apologizing for how she had been in November, saying let's meet, no, I can't, I'm sorry, and so on. She was coming back to him.

The next day she read the notes again, searching for the hint, the subtle declaration, no matter how guarded or tentative, that would reveal the nature of their affections. She could not find it. This must be the way historians feel, she reasoned, and crime lab investigators, archaeologists sweeping at the remains of a dig. Stumbling on the tiniest bit—the minimum, really—and forced to piece together a narrative, to fill in the gaps, though the evidence could be read to support any interpretation.

Of course, Ryan Whitehurst was doing the same out in LA. Or would be, soon enough. If news of his death hadn't reached her, possibly it never would, and she would be left to fashion her own tale, wondering what had happened, why Dale had stopped writing, whether he had decided to go back to being a husband or found someone else or what. A source of irritation and longing, yet she would keep watch all the while, scanning the lobbies at film festivals, the corridors in airports, sidewalks in certain cities, wondering if he would be there, if today would be the day.

She reviewed the events of the past year. If there had to be a reason for Dale to go out and see Ryan Whitehurst, to have an affair—the term *have an affair* struck her as odd and dated, but she could not think of a better one—then it certainly wasn't hard to find. In the months before he died they had been fighting all the time, over the most obvious, inescapable consideration. Children. She had told him she was ready, that it was time to start trying.

"You don't want children," was what he had said.

"I don't?"

"No. You don't want to regret not having children."

She didn't know how to respond. He was both right and not right. She had felt ready before only to watch the feeling recede, and became resistant; if everyone and everything—and that included her body—was telling her to do it, she was determined not to, to honor a more expansive and less conventional view of adulthood.

"With something as big as this," Dale said, "both people have to be on board."

"I know that. So are you neutral then, or positively against?"

"Positively against seems awful strong."

"So just against?"

"I don't know. I suppose."

Now and then they would pretend, discuss how parenting might work, how to manage their schedules and approach certain decisions. One time he let a pronoun slip.

"It would definitely be public school. He's not going to some white flight camp."

"He?" she teased.

"Honestly? I hope not."

But those times were rare. Usually he would say he was not ready. Or that she should finish her dissertation, and they could talk then.

"I am thinking of going off birth control," she told him one night.

"I am thinking of giving up sex."

She had considered counseling, feeling there was no other choice. It had got to the point where any attempt at communication, no matter how simple, was freighted. She yelled at him once because he forgot to fold a box before putting it in the recycling bin.

But after speaking to a receptionist, and copying down available appointment times, she could not bring herself to make one, unable to shake a recurrent fantasy. She could imagine the therapist sending her and Dale to separate rooms, telling them to write down their complaints and then asking, when they emerged, to exchange lists.

I wish you would listen to me. You just talk over what I'm saying, do the very thing you're accusing me of, and never reflect on that. You can't hear, you're totally disconnected from the major events in my life. We're trying to make this really important decision and all you do is think about yourself, your own needs.

That was her list. That was Dale's list. They had written down the same things.

Now she confronted the possibility that this was all beside the point, that it had nothing to do with Dale getting older or worrying about limits imposed on his freedom or any of the other motives she had ascribed to him. The truth was, he did not want to have children because he was in love with another woman.

Unless he was in love with another woman because he did not want to have children.

Reed said he would be unable to fly out after all.

"Now they want me to testify," he said. "Do a depo."

"A depo?"

"A pretrial interview or whatever."

"For this Ponzi thing?"

"Yes."

"You're going to be okay, aren't you?"

"On money? Sure. What's lost is lost, but only a small piece. Other people, not so much."

And he apologized again for missing the funeral, explaining why he couldn't be there, how after word of the scheme broke, and the first arrests made, there was a shakeup in the leadership of the company, vice presidents on the way out, more turnover to come, all of which had put him in charge of half the sessions at the retreat.

"On the other hand. Is it me, or is it really funny he had a funeral? A Catholic one I mean."

"No," she said, "it is funny. And I haven't even told you the best part. There's a plaque going up. Lucrece bought him real estate in the memorial chapel."

"A plaque? Can we go see it?"

"It's not up yet. There are some ashes to go in there too. I think she got a package rate. Listen, let me ask you something," she said. "I got this note from Ryan Whitehurst. Ever heard of her?"

There was a pause on the other end. She could not tell right away if it was significant or not.

"Ryan Whitehurst?"

"Yeah. She worked for a company called Atlas Productions."

"Sorry," said Reed. "Can't help you. Did she write out of the blue or what?"

"Sort of."

"And you invited her to the funeral?"

"No. You never heard of her?"

"What did her emails say?"

"Nothing important," Sandra said.

She told Richard Rawlings about the heist and sent him newspaper reports, which were not hard to find since one of those arrested was an athlete, a former tight end for the Giants. He had been the one to recruit investors, Reed included, for a shell company that made a series of fraudulent real estate deals.

"The trial starts in May," she told Richard Rawlings. "In lower Manhattan, though the attorneys are trying to get it moved."

“Sure,” he said, “but I don’t think Dale was wrapped up in that.”

“But you haven’t found them yet,” she said, meaning the shares from BAE.

“No. I’m sorry. It’s hard. You have to pursue all leads.”

“Can you give me an example,” she said. “Of a lead.”

“Too many to name. Finding a sum like this, it’s not large, it’s not nothing. A person’s life has so many nooks and crannies. It’s hard to believe, but when this is over, I’ll know your husband better than anyone.”

“Oh, I believe it,” she said.

Jealousy, she told herself, was not something she had a right to feel. Not anymore. When Dale died his passions died with him. No matter how unruly or errant they might have been.

And yet this reasoning did not make her feel better, not at all, and she began to wonder if it was jealousy that menaced her, or something else.

She had taken the wrong tack with Reed. It would have been better to confront him, to assume the affair as a given, and not even offer the chance to lie.

Because he had to have known. On reflection she did not believe him, did not believe he had never heard of Ryan Whitehurst, and she went back through Dale’s email, reading the notes they had sent to each other. There had to be some record of struggle, a tortured confession written at 2 or 3 a.m., Dale saying he couldn’t take it anymore, that he would have to forswear Ryan Whitehurst or ask Sandra for divorce.

In his emails to Reed she found nothing of the sort, so she began looking for references in code, alert to the hidden meaning of sentences like “Don’t plan on doing that, have danced with the devil too many times,” before realizing this was lunacy, its very definition, and there could be no end of it, to these questions and trapdoors of mystery. They would go on forever, a constant stream, obsession begetting obsession, and maybe she had been wrong to begin with, and there was no struggle. Maybe Dale liked seeing her every four or five months, liked how the affair would never grow stale that way, and there was no attempt to put it down, to curb it from his life. Maybe his death had been the only thing that could have stopped it.

She drove to Lighting Works, wondering if she should confide in Cheryl, or plumb her for information. Cheryl had slept with other men both while she was engaged and after, and Sandra wanted to know what it was like, the moment of decision, if in her case it had been accidental or headlong or the result of careful and searching reasoning, almost like computing a mathematical equation.

She found her working the bar, as she did from time to time to make a point to the staff, to show she did not consider herself above such menial work, and invited Nick, one of the newer bartenders, to join them. They ordered a Brewmaster Sampler and sat at one of the tables in the corner, in the same room where the funeral reception was held. The two had been talking about politics, Nick saying, "In our lifetime, there are two things we won't see: a Republican win the popular vote and the Senate flip Democrat."

"In our *lifetime*?" Cheryl answered.

"Mark my words."

"Kindly explain how you do your math."

Already Sandra was feeling the effects of the beer, and thinking about how the banter with Nick, the way they fenced like this, allowed Cheryl to see herself as she rarely could at home, in her marriage, as sassy and careless, a little wanton.

"It's the flyover," Nick continued. "It's all angry whites in the flyover. Not enough people to sway a national, but each of those states gets two seats."

Cheryl said with more women and people of color coming into the political system no assumptions were safe. "We've only ever had a government of white men."

"So? Power is power."

"You read that on a fortune cookie?"

"Maybe, but I meant it doesn't matter who's there. Temptation, corruption, are built into the job."

From here the conversation settled into a debate about the respective sins men and women were capable of. There was one point, Cheryl said, where she was perfectly ready to concede male superiority. "Men fuck and betray better," she said. "That's just a fact." And she mentioned politicians who had fathered illegitimate children or stored mistresses away on their staff.

"And those are just the ones we know about," she said, "so what does that tell you about the percentage overall?"

Now Sandra broke in, muttering something about secrets and double lives, how the dead can come back to haunt you.

Neither Nick nor Cheryl saw anything significant in the remark.

She drank two more pints, and when she got home tried to masturbate, but it misfired. It was not something she was expecting to find, but it turns out you cannot masturbate over the dead. Previously she had known limitless freedom in her sexual reveries, could jump back in time and be eighteen again, or copulate with gay men, and she was thinking of a night in Lucrece's minivan, when Dale told his parents they were going to a movie but instead turned down a long gravel road. They parked in front of a gate with a license plate bolted to it.

No one lives down here, he said. Not even when I was a kid.

But they were still jittery, not trusting the sound of twigs snapping or of frogs, and it was only when the windows fogged that they were able to go through with it.

She remembered the way Dale cupped her back, holding her up from the floor as he thrust, but could not bring herself to climax, and by the time she settled on another candidate, Sam Varner, the head of Audio-Visual at Clatsop, the impulse was spent. She was done.

With her underwear still around her ankles she reached for her phone. Sam Varner: she must have his number somewhere, buried at the bottom of an email. She found it, wrote a text, and stayed up another hour, waiting to hear from him, before passing out with the phone in her hand.

In the morning she stood with the French press at the island countertop in the kitchen. Scrolling through her texts, she had to laugh. Eleven thirty: that was when she sent it, and what could be funnier than her feigned nonchalance, the belief that somehow it was possible to say, "Hey would love to get a drink if you're around" at 11:30 on a weeknight and still maintain a veneer of cool.

Besides which, he never got it. Looking again at his email signature, she realized she had sent the text to his landline.

Later in the day she became nauseous and made it to the bathroom just in time, retching into the toilet, the crimson spittle dribbling across the floor.

She sat against the bowl, wiping her brow, trying to determine if this episode was like the others or simply a hangover. In the mirror of the closet she looked pale and sunken, and the scale, when she stepped on it, read 120. She had lost ten pounds since Dale died, and should have noticed this sooner, only she was wearing the same clothes, the same pocket tee and pajama bottoms, every day.

When she called the office of her primary care physician, she was told that no appointment was available until the end of the week, and the receptionist called again an hour later to say that unfortunately there had been an emergency and Dr. Channing would be unable to make any of his callbacks today.

Bereavement, vertigo: online she found an article that said Sertraline and Atarax were the recommended antidepressant regimen. Sandra had not heard of either but knew it was unlikely a physician would prescribe one of these over the phone.

Still, it should be today. She had to see someone today. She took the card she had been given at the funeral reception out of the basket by the refrigerator.

The Best Day Clinic was located in a corner of the waterfront that was under construction. She crossed a pier at the end of the parking lot, the land beneath gullied out, with walls of dirt spaded flat and cement pylons stacked in a pyramid. Yet the lobby of the warehouse was finished, with small bulbs in pastel shades dancing across sculptures and an installation made from the jaws of an old docking elevator.

She passed the doors for a skin care center and an investment firm before coming to a bulletin board that displayed posters for crisis centers. Bulimia, alcoholism, suicide prevention. Beside this was a dry-erase board with class notes and reminders on them. "Thursday 7:00'ers, bring your notebook" and "Ray's birthday gathering Friday sunrise meet at parking lot." There was also a collection of what Sandra guessed were testimonials or exit statements, endorsements.

The friends I made here I will have forever.

Thanks to Best Day I can see life again.

Inside she found a room furnished like an elementary school, with a circle of chairs around a low table and a blackboard on an easel. Charcoal sketches of the harbor, a shelf with initials printed by a label gun. In the back a cinderblock wall reached halfway to the ceiling, and in the corner was a pottery wheel, the brackets smeared with daubings of paint. Sandra picked up the block of clay that was on the seat, the silt cold and striped from the borings in the wheel, fingerprints covering one end, a smattering of concentric rings like a topographical map.

She sat on the board that was wedged between the sides and put her foot on the pedal to get the wheel going. Before she could do anything more she heard a voice, and going out the other end of the storage cubby saw a wall of glass in front of a smaller room, what must have been an office in the time when this was a warehouse. Three people were sitting at desks, their heads bowed, with paper in front of them, and every so often they stopped what they were writing or drawing to listen to a prompt delivered by a woman in a navy cardigan and slacks, who stood with her back to Sandra. She tried to get out before being seen, but it was too late, and the woman turned and waved and gave one more set of instructions before opening the door.

"May I help you, ma'am?"

"I'm sorry. I didn't realize you had a class. I was not trying to intrude."

"Don't you worry about that now. Tell me how I can help you."

"Are you Jenny Travers?" she asked, and the woman nodded and pointed to the table and Sandra followed her and sat down. The edge brushed against her shins, and she tapped on the surface with her knuckles. "What's this," she said, "some cutting-edge therapy technique?"

"A low table brings out your inner child?"

"Or helps stave off conflict. Whatever."

"I wish. No, most of the stuff you see here was donated."

"I see. Well, again, I'm sorry to have interrupted. Your husband, that's why I'm here. He knew my husband. Dale Tobin. Do you know about Dale Tobin?"

"Yes. I'm sorry. Yes, I remember that name. Is that why you came in? Tuesday is our regular class for widows."

"That's not what I'm interested in."

"No?"

"No. I'm looking for someone to talk to because I keep having these fits. Dizziness, mostly. And nausea, my heart rate. And I need to know." She stopped. "I need to know if this is real or something I'm imagining."

"Why would you be imagining it?"

"That's what people do, isn't it? Make themselves sick to take their minds off trauma."

"That's a new one on me. What was the last meal you ate?"

Sandra tried to remember. Cheryl had taken her to a food truck earlier in the week and she had eaten a taco, or half a taco. Almost half. That and cabbage on the side. Cabbage and salsa.

"It's probably the best thing for a doctor to look at. Not me. A clinician. You understand that."

"I do," Sandra replied. "I can't get an appointment."

"There's always urgent care."

"Yes. There always is."

"Preferably before it happens again."

"Who's this, a new quack?"

It was one of the students, or one of the patients, who said this. She had come out of the room, shuffling slightly, and was studying Sandra, her expression intent, almost leering. The woman's hair was down and her face spotted, as if from windburn, her hoodie drenched in cigarette smoke.

"Lee," Jenny said, "time is not up."

"I know. I'm finished."

She held out a sheet of paper covered with a sloping penmanship.

"That's good," said Jenny. "Thank you. Now please go back and wait."

"I just wanted to meet our new friend. Jeez."

"Sandra is not enrolled in the class."

"So why are you here?"

Sandra was surprised to be addressed directly, when it seemed the custom was for Jenny to act as intermediary in all conversations. She said, "I'm just visiting."

"Yeah, that's what I'm doing too. Funny. We both use the same excuse."

"Lee is one of our newest visitors at Best Day," Jenny said.

"Don't say it like that. You sound like you're on Prozac when you say it. Seriously now," she turned back to Sandra, "what's your problem?"

"I told you she's not a patient," said Jenny.

"A shrink?"

"No."

"Then what?"

"She just helps out from time to time."

Jenny turned back to the room walled in glass. Sandra did not see what it was, but one of the others—a woman dressed in a long sweater folded across her chest like a serape, and a man with a pudgy face and a vacant or sheepish look—must have made some sort of signal, obliging her to get up and check on them.

"What days do you work?" Lee asked once she was gone, taking her seat.

"What?"

"Jenny said you were helping out. So when?"

"I don't really work here," Sandra said. "I'm just a graduate student."

"A what?"

"I study fossils. Read and write about them."

"Trust fund baby?"

"I wish. I also teach, filmmaking and theater, at Clatsop."

"Pretty cush life."

Sandra shrugged and made a tiny motion with her hands as Jenny came back into the room.

"Now Lee, please say goodbye to Sandra. We're moving on to part two. Come. Bring your paper. We'll be doing a circular exchange."

"Hell no."

"Lee, we've talked about this. Step one is to accept the structure of the class. It's not fair to everyone. It isn't fair if we don't all have buy-in."

"Fine then. I got my partner right here."

"No," said Jenny. "Sandra was just about to leave. Weren't you, Sandra?"

"Come on," Lee said. "You think I like talking to the other drunks? 'Hey Randy, that's a nice painting'—it's not—'I love the bulbs you made in the foreground'—I thought they were shoes—'keep working at it and show me the next one'—please get me out of here before I shoot myself in the face. I'm just here because of the lawyers. I'd rather talk to you if you're not a therapy person. If you're a real person."

"I can stay for a bit," Sandra said. "It's okay. I don't mind."

Jenny closed her eyes, put a hand on her chest and inhaled slowly, then began to describe the exercise, speaking loudly enough that the other two members of the class could also hear. If part one had been titled "Bricks," she said, this second half was "Balloons." Your partner was to read what you wrote and write a new version of it. A version without names, without pronouns.

That way the characters would be given a more equal footing, the audience would not automatically be led to favor one over the other, yet both might be validated and rendered with sympathy.

"The idea is to learn how to privilege communication that goes beyond assigning blame," Jenny said. "You can't forgive yourself if you never figure out how to forgive others. And vice versa. It's time to write a new story. Your partner can help."

It sounded sensible enough, Sandra considered, though the name was ridiculous. Bricks and balloons. It was like a graphic you might see on television, to teach children shapes and letters.

"When I wrote this, I thought it was going to be private," Lee said after Jenny had walked away. She handed Sandra the sheet of paper. On it was the Lord's Prayer and the lyrics to "Deck the Halls."

"It started off being a letter to my husband," she said. "But I got writer's block. Too much material. Too much to work with."

"Your husband. What does he do?"

"Sits on his ass. Trades SNAP funds for cash. And that's ex-husband I should say."

"Why don't you tell me one thing?"

"One thing."

"Yeah. What the letter was going to say." If ever there was someone who had the fulminating gift, Sandra thought, the ability to author a memorable screed right on the spot, first draft, no revisions, that person was probably Lee.

"You ever been married?" Lee said.

"Yes."

"Well then. What would you say?"

"What would I say?"

"Yeah. You're so curious about me. What's your letter to your husband?"

"We're not married anymore," Sandra said.

"Ex-husband. Whatever."

"What would I say to him? I don't know. There's nothing I would regret or take back about the marriage. Nothing I did. What I would take back would be what I thought of it, how I judged my own position. The computation was off. All along I thought my marriage was only an incidental part of my life. Something important, yes, but also on the side. Not all of it. Not the core of me."

"And?"

"And that's it. That's my brick, that's what I would ask forgiveness for. Are you going to rewrite it?"

"I don't know how you're supposed to rewrite that. It's pretty lame. All you're giving me is a thought, and I don't see how you can be apologizing for a thought."

"Thoughts are deeds," Sandra said. "Are they not?"

"Thoughts are what?"

"Well for some there is no distinction. To think a crime, or to dream it, is to commit it."

"I don't know what to tell you," said Lee, "except in that case we're all going to hell. I'll see you there."

When she got home she phoned Jenny at Best Day and said, "I didn't really know what to do. The whole time I was worried about making a blunder, some terrible breach of protocol."

"No, it's my fault," Jenny said. "When I said you were helping out here. I was just trying to protect you."

"I told her talking to me isn't going to help much. Am I right about that?"

"Yes. Deirdre and I—the other person who runs Best Day—give a full report of any treatment, once the program is fulfilled. Typically that's a month or eight meetings. A week. Something. And Lee hasn't sat through one. Until today. I suppose she gets credit for today."

Sandra wanted to ask why Lee was going to Best Day, though she knew Jenny couldn't tell her. She had mentioned booze—the other drunks, that was what she had said—and there must be something else at work, drugs or the occasional manic episode. Unless Lee had just decided there was no sense trying to manage the unmanageable. Her own slant on grief. Putting on a face, pretending to normalcy, waiting for the resumption of before when there was no before: once you quit all that, Sandra thought, maybe there was nothing to do except live as Lee was, scattershot, a live wire.

"I'd like to help," she went on, "but I can't keep coming back every day. Or every week, whatever it is."

"No. Of course not."

"Right, so I'll talk to her and try to coax her back to the main group."

"If you really want to do that to yourself," said Jenny. "And hey."

"Yes?"

"Go to the doctor."

She did not go to the doctor. Instead she looked at the list the contractor had made. She could not replace the backsplash in the kitchen, or the copper pipe leaking above the ceiling panel, but she could install a new patio door and paint the walls upstairs, clean up the basement and get it ready for showing.

She found an old oxford that belonged to Dale and used that to work in, pulling free a dry cleaner's tag that was pinned to the lower button.

In the basement nothing had been touched in a year or more. It was like stepping into a house that was not her own, that had been abandoned in a time of nuclear fallout, the ladder still open in front of the circuit box, notes stuck to the ceiling beams, screwdrivers fitted between staples. In a pool of sawdust she recognized Dale's boot print. Birds had wintered beneath the Bilco doors, building a nest with strips of tinsel and a candy bar wrapper. And there were castoffs, things she and Dale found when moving in they had not bothered to dispense with. An air-conditioning unit, a portable camping stove.

There were always trucks, Dale told her once. Out scouting for scrap metal, for anything with copper in it. She brought the air-conditioner to the curb. Within five minutes a pickup had come to take it away. So she brought some deck chairs out there as well, a futon and set of filing cabinets.

None of her neighbors said a word. It was the bliss of being a widow. Or it would be bliss, if she were not a widow. For two months, maybe more, she was out of bounds. There was nothing she could do against the social grain and draw a reprimand. Dress in a leather suit, a Catwoman outfit. Stand on the corner in nothing but a sandwich board.

She should do more, in all honesty, to take advantage of it.

Later in the week the city left a calendar in her mailbox showing collection days, with the list of approved items for landfill circled in marker.

She finished the upstairs first, covering the furniture with curtains and a table runner and a bolt of muslin she used to wrap silverware in. She painted the walls Wisteria Snow, a shade Beth recommended, and smoothed cracks with a tube of patch. When she stopped by to take photos of the house, Beth said, "Beautiful, it looks just like a professional would have done. And I have a present for you."

She took out a sign that said Coming Soon and placed it in the middle of the circular drive.

"I know you did not want to do this," Sandra said.

"Oh no," said Beth, running her finger along a beam in the porch. "No, we're way past that. We're going to get this done."

On one of the nights she was painting Cheryl left a message, saying, "I drove by and saw some lights on. I tried texting but think you might only be answering calls."

Sandra pressed seven to delete the message and walked into the kitchen and stood with her hands on the countertop. She was looking at her phone, the screenshot a photo of Dale's, taken in the Pyrenees, the mountainside banked in mist. Her uncle who lived in Pau had bought a house there, one that was said to have been used by the Gestapo during the war for interrogation. When the screen faded, she put her hand to it to keep it from going black and turned and opened the refrigerator. Inside the door was a bottle of prosecco Dale had bought for New Year's, only they learned one of Cheryl's friends was planning to make a similar drink—Dale's recipe called for citrus and St. Germain—so they had left it at home. She twisted in the corkscrew and poured a glass and dialed her voicemail again. She had not listened to the messages yet. She thought if she had to, she could hold out for another week, yet she also felt now was the time to do it. Do it and stop thinking about it.

There were three of them saved. In the first Dale read the model number on a set of tires and asked if she could find a lower price. In the second nothing save the click of the connection ending. She could not remember why she had saved it, only that at some date in the future she planned to remember and did not want to regret erasing it. After a beat she heard Dale's voice again.

"Hi sweetheart. This is Dale. Well, duh."

"And Reed too. Don't forget. Hi Sandra!"

"And we're where, thirteen thousand feet?"

"Really fucking high," Reed said. "Too high."

"We trekked away from the bar and through the snow to be able to say happy birthday from the top of the world." Then, and she could tell he was talking to Reed, holding the phone away from him, "What time is it?"

"My phone's cracked."

"Reed's been complaining all day," said Dale, louder, back into the phone. "He fell on his snowboard. I got it. Ready? Three, two, one, happy birthday!"

And they yelled in unison for the rest of the message.

She had gone to bed by the time they called and turned her ringer off. She spoke to Dale earlier, around eight o'clock. "Happy birthday," he said then. "My present is waiting for you at home."

"I know where," she said. And she did, too. He always hid presents in the storage closet in the garage.

She pressed nine to save the message and drank the prosecco and was about to call Reed and share it with him but stopped.

There was something else. What? It passed before her, indecipherable, and passed again.

He had emailed Ryan Whitehurst about it. Sandra was almost positive. She went back to his account to check.

> Shooting in Whistler, not the resort but one of the mountains behind it, following this band of snowboarders who I guess are also a cult. They're Bolivian, trace their roots back to some tribe there. Tacking on a few days at the end, a friend is flying out.

No doubt he was texting her in the bar. Impossible that he wouldn't, being with Reed, drinking, unless he was observing some silent code of conduct, saying no, I will not do it on Sandra's birthday.

Either way she would have to delete the message. Hearing it, she wouldn't be able to think of anything except Ryan Whitehurst. She played it again, and this time, when it was finished, she hit seven.

It was all going to be like this, she saw. Nothing was safe now, nothing inviolate. She was in a state of freefall.

She backed up, hoping to find a memory that was free of the contaminant of Ryan Whitehurst, and settled on the first trip down the Pacific Coast Highway.

"Want to come with?"

The days when Dale had seemed like her double. By the time he died each knew they were not, but there was no regret in the way things had turned out. Each believed they had given up certain similarities in order to enjoy something larger. A marriage built on a hidden and more fundamental compatibility.

Yet who, after all, was Ryan Whitehurst but another version of the person Sandra had been in her twenties—a cinephile, unencumbered. The profile was unmistakable, even down to the bag they had, the clutch. Dale was still searching for his double.

Perhaps this was the lesson of grief, the thing you saw after scaling the mountain and getting over the clouds, that people were the sum of their secrets, and when they died there was no picking the lock, for they took it with them. The tintype and ankle bracelet, the password and answers to the security questions. The sale of stock. And now the email, the horror deriving not from jealousy but the threat of nullification. To find out the most intimate thing in your life—your marriage—was also the most alien. That all you thought was, was not.

The next time Sandra showed up at Best Day, class was already in session. Behind the door she heard music, the piping of flutes, and Jenny's voice counting down from five. Some slogan or promise was recited in unison. She waited in the lobby, but Lee did not show. Sandra thought she may already be inside, and when she went to the door again, she saw a note on the dry-erase board. It had been written by Jenny.

Sandra: Lee called and wanted to tell you she's at Porter's. JT

Porter's, if Sandra was thinking of the right place, was a coffee shop several blocks away, at the end of a small wharf. She got lost trying to find it. There was no path or alley between the warehouses, and she had to pass through a makeshift tunnel and go under the construction zone before coming to a staircase that led up the hill and back to the street. By the time she got to Porter's she hoped Lee was gone, but she found her at one of the tables in the back, watching a movie on her phone.

"Lee, what is this? I never said I would meet you here."

"I know."

"Do you?"

"Hey, don't talk to me like that."

"I never said we were coming here. We have to stay at Best Day."

"That sounds like a poem. We have to stay at Best Day, where the air is fine and there's never wine."

Her hair was up, and with it pulled back Sandra could see there were auburn streaks in it. Instead of the hoodie she wore a lavender tee, the sleeves cut off at the shoulders. Sandra was amazed by the difference, by how young she looked. It was a face that said there was time still—plenty of time still.

"You don't get credit if you don't sit with the others. I told you, I'm not a professional."

"Good for you. You're not a professional. I'm so happy about that. But I can't go to the booby hatch today."

She jutted her chin at the corner of the restaurant, where there was a girl kneeling on a grid of plastic squares with letters of the alphabet written on them, rummaging through a bucket with rope handles. The sign above her said "UNATTENDED CHILDREN WILL BE GIVEN CAFFEINE."

Sandra took off her jacket and sat down.

"What's her name?"

"Tina. The one and only."

Sandra watched her pull a dump truck out of the bucket and make a whooshing noise as if dirt or gravel was spilling out of the back.

"Last time you said something about lawyers," she said.

"I don't have a lawyer. Assface tried to get one. After my arrest. Hoping I'd fold. Please."

"Your arrest?"

"Totally rigged. I had like one beer. They pull me over for the light and I said, no, I'm getting it checked, and I had the receipt even, I showed it to them, said here, and they ask if I've been drinking. Not one word about the light. So then it's a DUI. Later I get the summons, and I thought it was a mistake but no, there was another one for the taillight. I keep waiting for them to try me for the Kennedy assassination."

"And she was with you, wasn't she?" said Sandra. "When you were pulled over."

"Yeah she was with me. So what? I said it was one beer. But the mediator told me to get help. He said no custody agreement would get approved unless I went to a Best Day kind of place."

"Well you better go, Lee. Seriously. Don't miss today. Go. I can watch her."

"You? Do you have any experience with children?"

"None. But this seems like a pretty well-supervised place. I don't think I can get away with any crimes here."

She reached into her purse and took out one of Dale's business cards. Underneath the logo for Vestiture was their address. She wrote her phone number on the back.

"Give it to the police if we're gone," she said.

"Funny. I don't know what to tell her."

"Don't tell her anything. Just go. You won't even be an hour. I got it."

Lee took her sweater off the chair and lingered at the exit, between the doors, until Sandra fluttered her hand. A moment later she saw her drive out of the lot, and moved her chair closer to Tina, who seemed to be no older than four or five, her hair blond, combed back and held into place by a butterfly pin, its wings jade or crystal. She pushed the dump truck to the edge of the alphabet squares.

A voice from the counter calling out an order number caused Tina to look at the table where Lee had been sitting. Sandra stood and waved to her.

"Your mommy had to run an errand," she said. "She'll be right back."

Tina looked at her with the middle fingers of her left hand in her mouth.

"My name is Sandra. Or Sammy. That's what people called me when I was your age."

"Sammy the turtle?"

"No. It was just easier to say, or remember. You know, I like your dress. Can you tell me what it is? It looks like a rocket ship."

Tina pulled the front of it down so Sandra could see the design. Above the sparkles and beaded hoops around the waist was an orange cone with a flag painted on top and flames bordering the flanged sides.

"I'm hungry," Tina said, and put the fingers back in her mouth.

"Perfecto," Sandra said. "Let's see what they have."

She led Tina to the cooler.

"What's that?" Tina was pointing at one of the cups.

"Lemonade."

"I want that. I want lemonade."

"Does your mommy let you have lemonade?" Sandra swirled the cup around. "There's a lot of sugar in this," she said.

"I want it, I want it."

"Fine. What else."

But Tina had already run off with the lemonade. She drank it on the edge of the playpen and removed the parts of a racetrack from the bucket, joining some red and beige slabs together and attaching other components, a dugout with the words Body Shop painted over it and a pump to simulate a gas station.

Sandra said, "I can show you how to work that if you want."

"Shhh." Tina put a finger to her lips and removed a kit of jacks from the bucket, and a plastic dinosaur and some logs, and she took out several more toys before settling on a small furry knob, a mouse or bunny, with stiff whiskers and a pair of rounded ears. She slid it into the grooves of the track.

"Sweetheart, that's not going to run," Sandra said. "It doesn't have wheels."

Tina did not answer but placed the jacks at intervals inside the track and spread some of the logs around them. To Sandra it seemed like she was piling up toys indiscriminately, until she understood the racetrack was not a racetrack. It was meant to be a fence bounding a garden or woods, the bunny crawling around in hopes of finding a way out, the story altering whenever it encountered a new object, the dinosaur, for instance, now made to represent a scarecrow, and one corner of the racetrack becoming a tunnel through which it was possible to escape into the bucket. "Meanwhile," Tina would say, narrating, or "but" to preface a further development, and Sandra knew there was a certain logic at play, the logic of narrative in its infant or seedling form. Unforeseen problems, delayed resolution: Tina already understood that a story must first have a rhythm, a texture and pattern of rise and fall, before it could have anything else.

Tina exchanged the mouse or bunny for one of the cars, and Sandra got up and ordered a cinnamon roll at the counter. She cut the bun into small pieces and tasted one to make sure it wasn't too hot.

"Sweetheart, can you try this?" she said, holding out a fork. "Your mom's going to be back soon, and I think it will make her happy if you ate something."

"I'm not hungry."

"You said you were."

"I'm not."

"You don't even want to try it?"

Tina squinted, a slight downturn at the edges of her mouth, and Sandra saw the welt appear, a small darkening at first, then spilling across one thigh. She picked her up at the waist, the warmth of the urine seeping into her sweater, and carried Tina to the bathroom and took off her dress and her stockings and shoes. She rubbed her arms to make sure she wasn't shivering. The skin soft, as unblemished as candlewax.

"Sweetheart, you wait here and Sammy's going to be back in two seconds, okay?"

She did not want to leave her, yet she had no choice, and went out and asked the first waitress she saw for a change of clothes.

"Anything you can find," she said.

In the bathroom Tina was crying. Sandra held her close. She said, "Oh no, sweetheart, it's okay, it happens all the time," only now Sandra was crying too, cupping Tina's head, holding her so hard the butterfly pin fell out. She told herself it was nothing. Just an accident, no reason to fall prey, yet again, to the distorting effects of mourning. Bruising too easily, seeing all events, even this one, as a cataclysm. Yet for the longest while she couldn't stop, and realized it was the first time she had done this, broken down, since the night of Dale's accident. At last Tina wriggled free of her grasp.

"Sammy, what is it?"

Sandra took a paper towel from the dispenser. She was about to say "it's been a hard month" when she started to laugh, picturing herself blubbering on like this in the presence of a four-year-old.

Soon she was laughing with the same abandonment with which she had been sobbing only moments before.

There was a knock, and when Sandra opened the door the waitress handed her a plastic bag.

"There's also this," she said.

The Oregon Ducks shirt was a kid's size, 4T, but it fell over Tina like a nightie. Inside the bag was an apron. She knotted it around the shirt so no one would see Tina wasn't wearing underclothes and then took the pair of pink covers like surgical clogs out of the bag and slipped them on Tina's feet and found a roll of duct tape beneath the sink and bit off a piece to tie the slack together around the heels.

"All right," she said. "You look like you're ready to scrub in. Surgery, nine o'clock."

She stuffed the wet clothes into the bag and smoothed Tina's hair behind her ears, holding it in place with the butterfly pin.

"This'll be our secret, okay? Don't tell mommy Sammy started to cry. And I won't tell her about the lemonade. Promise? We're partners now."

A few hours later Lee texted to say not all of Tina's clothes were in the bag. Sandra drove back to Porter's, and the same waitress found Tina's stockings in a bin in the kitchen. Sandra took them home and put them in the wash. The address Lee gave her was 421 Butte Farms. Sandra was expecting a subdivision or apartment complex, but Butte Farms turned out to be a trailer park tucked away on one of the flats near the harbor, the mobile homes and double-wides arrayed on a winding grid of streets, and she had to circle back almost to the highway before she found the right one, screened from the road by a stand of pines.

No one seemed at home. She stood on the cinderblock stair, ringing the doorbell, and then went around to the back, where she found Lee on a camping chair, smoking in front of a space heater hooked up to an extension cord.

"I'll bring these in for you," she said, and held up the clothes. Inside the trailer she moved her hand around the wall until realizing there were no switch for the light and instead reached for the string that hung from a glass shade. The bedroom and kitchen were on opposite sides, and a few toys were scattered on the orange shag, a can of Play-Doh and a tin astronaut, but Tina did not seem to have her own room or play area. Sandra left the clothes on top of a chest that looked like it might be a laundry hamper.

"Tina's not here?" she said, opening the door.

"You see her?" Lee said. She slapped the cigarettes against one hand and flicked the pack with her wrist and bent to grab one with her teeth. "She's gone to Chu's," she said, lighting it and leaning back and nodding into the distance.

Sandra did not know who that was. "What do you do during the daytime?" she said. "If you don't mind me asking."

"Bring her to the office with me. It's just answering phones, so. And I got a friend, LuAnn, who works the Mini Mart nights."

"Jesus, Lee. What about school?"

"Not until next year. Another brilliant move by our government. Win a September 3 birthday and you know what you get? You get to wait a whole fucking year. Three hundred and sixty-three days."

"Do you want me to take another crack at it?" Sandra said. "I will."

Lee nodded and let out a cloud of smoke.

"What about them fossils?"

"Well. Lord knows I have the time."

"And I guess your husband isn't around to bother you none."

"No," Sandra said. "He's not."

The following week Lee called to ask Sandra if she could take Tina to the doctor. The appointment was on Tuesday. "It's nothing fancy," Lee said. "Just a checkup, but let me know if you want to wimp out."

Sandra borrowed a car seat from one of Cheryl's friends. She wondered if what she was doing was legal or whether she was violating certain privacy protections by bringing Tina to the clinic. But the nurse asked for nothing save Lee's address, and once Sandra provided it, she led them to the corridor outside the examination rooms. Sandra was relieved to hear there were no immunizations, and Tina accepted the consultation as a challenge, batting Sandra away when she tried to help her onto the scale and insisting on being the one to hold the wooden stick over her eye. Sandra could not make out the shapes—the pointer was down to the lowermost rows of the chart—but Tina answered, "An apple, a house, an umbrella," and sat dutifully on the chair, her legs high off the floor, as her blood pressure was measured.

On their way out the receptionist said, "It's going to be twenty, okay?"

"What?"

"Twenty dollars is your copay."

Sandra had never paid for a doctor's visit before. She assumed insurance would take care of it and wondered if this was why Lee had wanted Sandra to take her—if she had been too timid or ashamed to ask for money.

From the appointment they drove to a bookstore and wandered around while waiting for story hour to start. On one of the tables Sandra saw a guide, *So You're Thinking of Having a Child?*, that she had almost bought for Dale, a year before, and paging through it she was struck by how easily the text could double as a how-to for widows. All you had to do was change the covers. Change the titles. Leave everything else, the tips on how to manage cravings, how to recognize mood swings. It was all the same, the hormonal flares and waves of nausea, the stabs of remorse and guilt.

She tried to find something for Tina, but it was not easy guessing what she would like. There were so many characters and series, Sandra could not keep up with them all. There was Biscuit and the Hungry Caterpillar, Paw Patrol and *How Do Dinosaurs*, while the books from Sandra's own youth were in a section labeled Classics. Reading them again, after thirty years, she was surprised to discover how many were exhortative, the story unfolding in such a way as to disclose some lesson in manners. *Ferdinand the Bull*, for instance, was really about the virtues of docility. Pacifism rewarded. And when she looked at a reissue of the first volume of *Curious George*, she found it sinister, unintentionally sinister, the book an allegory about the African slave trade. Some artifact of the antebellum South, the flesh trader—the man in the yellow hat—treated as paternalistic and wise.

Tina tried to lift a stargazing atlas. Sandra caught it just as it was about to fall on her feet.

"This is nice," she said, opening one of the foldouts, "but you don't really read it. It's more like a map. There's not much of a story."

"I want to read it."

"There aren't even captions on a lot of the pages."

"What?"

"Nothing. Here, I'll give it a go."

Sandra tried to relate the tale of Cassiopeia, but all she could remember was that the queen was in love with her own beauty.

"And in this way she made someone mad," she said to Tina.

"Who?"

"A god no doubt. Or a king, a halfway god, with thunderbolts coming out of his hands and such. He punished her."

"Because she thought she was beautiful?"

"No, you're right. There had to be some ancillary reason. Another suitor. She moved in on someone who was married to the god and got caught and was banished. Sent to the skies. When we look up at night, we see her." She moved her thumb over the constellation. "Those are the stars, that's Cassiopeia, and these letters and slashes are the coordinates. Plug them into a telescope and you'll see her."

"That's what my dad makes."

"He makes what, sweetheart?"

"Scopes."

Sandra wondered if she was talking about rifles. "Scopes," she said, "what are those?"

"So you can see the stars."

"Telescopes."

Tina put two fingers in her mouth and nodded.

"So do you want to get this book?" she said. "We can get it and Sammy will learn the stories for real. We'll learn them together. Like a project. Okay?"

From the bookstore they came out onto Grand Avenue. There was some kind of parade or race going on, and she had to detour around Highway 30 before approaching the road again from the north. As traffic started to thin out, she moved over to pass a pickup when the vehicle made to turn. Its signal was not on, and she stepped on the brake and the coupe fishtailed into the opposite lane. They missed a delivery van by no more than a few feet and she heard a horn like one of those that come out of the harbor in a fog and looked to see the hood of a semi floating into the windshield, the figurine on top of the radiator an eagle carved out of steel or pewter, its wings folded down like a cloak. She steered the wheel to the right. The car brushed up against another veering into the turn lane, and she steered again and they coasted down a side street until the front tire hit the curb and she pulled on the emergency brake.

"Sammy."

Her chest was heaving. Above the trees was a sign for a gas station, and she saw it three times, the letters puddled, blurry shapes seen through 3D goggles. She drew in a lungful of air and counted to five.

"Sammy?"

"Yes, sweetheart?"

"What are we doing?"

"Just taking a break. How are you feeling, do you feel okay?"

"I heard the beat," Tina said.

She wiped the moisture from her forehead and adjusted the rearview back into place. "Say again sweetheart," she said.

"I heard the beat."

She realized Tina was talking about the hearing test, when the nurse gave her some headphones and asked if she would raise a finger when she heard a ping in her right or left ear.

"You did, you did hear the beat," she said, and put the car into gear. Before leaving she tested her vision by concentrating on the handles on a telephone pole and making sure they didn't waver. And she avoided the highway, thinking she knew the way to Butte Farms, yet it soon became apparent she was lost. At an intersection she paused. While entering the address on her phone she began to read the sign that was posted outside a church. "A Bible in the hand is better than two on the bookcase." She had seen this before, or something like it. She was sure. A slogan on the marquee, next to worship times for the week. "Don't give up—Moses was once a basket case." Instead of turning right, as the GPS told her, she went straight, expecting there to be a sign, though there was none. She had an image in her mind, of the straightness of the road and the sudden appearance of a clearing, closing in again on a glade of birch. She drove another mile and turned around, backtracking to a fork. This time she took the other side of it, and then they were at the right field.

"See those stones?" she said to Tina, turning toward the car seat. "Glaciers left those. Mountains of ice. A long time ago. Though some people think they were brought by outer space people."

"Outer space people?"

"Yes."

"That was their house?"

"If you believe that sort of thing."

It was true. Many persisted in believing the boulders were some alien handprint. A conference one year was devoted to the question, and Channel 8 had hired Dale to film the stones, the segment titled "Oldest Remaining Mystery in Oregon." They did not send anyone for assistant camera, so Sandra had gone to help him, positioning the dolly in front of the largest boulder and panning across while careful to keep Venus, showing already at three or four in the afternoon, in the shot.

How could she have forgotten this. Or Moses was once a basket case. Or the traffic. It was so stalled, going back, they had considered driving to Portland to deliver the footage. When they got home and were able to upload it, they had minutes to spare. Ten at the most.

"When did the aliens live here?" Tina asked.

"A long time ago, sweetheart. Or maybe not. Maybe in the eighties. Truthfully, I don't really know. It's just what some people believe."

All of town might be littered with such clues, like a map whose signposts were hidden, capable of being discovered only with a cipher or through the application of some reagent. Memory, this month had taught her, had a way of becoming grooved, the same words and sensations looped, on infinite repeat. There was only so much of him she could bring back on her own, and she would go for long drives, purposelessly, with no end in sight. The trick was to turn off her mind, disobey intention, take random turns off the highway and wait for the buried moment to assert itself. On a billboard whose corners had peeled off so she could see parts of the vinyl below was a faded advertisement for batteries, and for some reason—it must be the names, she reflected, they must rhyme—she thought of Kettle chips, and a morning when they stopped at a rest station on their way to the airport. While she was in the bathroom Dale had gone to the vending machines, and as they pulled back onto the on-ramp he remarked on how strange it was that here, of all places, he could find this brand of chips. And even something as simple as this, a bag of Kettle chips, brought its comet tail of reliving and association, for she also remembered being stuck on the runway later that morning, and the delay with the de-icing truck, running through the next terminal to make their connection. Dale hung back, refused to move faster than a trot, saying, "They won't close the door. They'll see on the computer we're delayed. They know we're coming."

She was not sure if what had happened with Tina in the car was a panic attack, but after the day they almost collided with the truck she became determined to gain weight. She switched grocery stores, frequenting a co-op on the west end of town that she and Dale belonged to but rarely visited, and bought foods she never had when he was alive, chard and nectarines and goat's milk, and downloaded an app that told her what to eat and when. A smoothie at 4:10, chicken and rice at 7:00. She would not eat unless so ordered.

Beth had scheduled some private showings, and said it would be better if Sandra was not there. She thought about leaving town altogether, driving down the coast and checking into a motel with a cheap weekly rate. Where the rooms opened off a wide hallway with a shared bathroom at one end, and the stairs buckled from being exposed to decades of salt air. No air-conditioning but heavy iron steam vents in the rooms, dumbwaiters that dropped into the kitchen, and a view of the boardwalk, of the rides and seaside attractions shuttered for the winter.

Instead she dug out her source work, the scans of trace fossils and maps that showed the coastline of Oregon as it evolved millennia ago. She took out a carrel in the library but couldn't find her way back in, and all the other times when the dissertation had stalled Dale had been there to pull her out. She had been able to finish only when he put her on a quota, two hundred fifty words a day. Every evening he would read the new page aloud, finding something in it to praise.

"I feel like a kid," she said on one of those nights, "like a kid and you're giving me a happy gram."

Now when she read the manuscript, everything seemed wrong. The structure, the transitions between chapters. She would have to write her adviser and ask for more time, and yet what would she do with an extension but go on parsing the same studies and quarreling with the existing literature like any good academic? Just more of the same solitary madhouse enterprise. And no one was waiting for it. That was the worst part. She knew what her adviser's answer would be. Of course she could have an extension. It didn't matter what she did. If she finished, fine. If not, also fine.

She began to scan job openings. Some of her friends had sent notices or referred her for film gigs—jobs she did not think she would have been offered if Dale had not been killed. Line producer on a feature. Second unit director for a documentary shoot of the Sea to Sky Highway. Her friends, no doubt, were thinking it would be good to get out of the house and join a crew. By the first day she would realize how much she missed it and would be grateful for the distraction. But no. She could not tell them this—she had barely told Dale this—but the filmmaking impulse was not like some flame you could bend down and blow on and cup your hand around and shield from the wind and wait for it slowly to revive. It had gone out of her; when, she was not quite sure of, but it was gone for good.

There were other, more bizarre solicitations. In her inbox was a message from Wesley Bruce. She could not remember anyone by that name, yet evidently he had known her, or at least known Dale. The first sentence of his note was about having time on her hands, and the link he gave was to an organization called the Media Policy Initiative. He mentioned that applications were coming open for the post of communications director, yet his description sounded like it was written by a bot, some claptrap about media being a tool to transform society, bridge communities—she did not even bother to read all of it.

No, her best chance would be a stopgap, a visiting professorship, replacing a faculty member who had gone on sabbatical. Those positions generally did not come open until April or May, but she was able to find two now, in both listings the proviso she coveted, the department accepting ABD candidates at the associate professor level.

One of these schools was in Pittsburgh, and as she drew up the cover letter she also began looking at real estate. Most of what she saw she couldn't afford. Tudors in Squirrel Hill, single-family co-ops in Oakland. Pressing the minus key in the lower right corner of the map, she scrolled to other locations, forty miles or more away. Cabins that were off the grid, with a privy instead of an indoors bath, and acreage with an abandoned silo and other outbuildings on it, which would appeal only to developers. She clicked on the photos of one, a camp that had been used by a fishing company or contracted to a state park, three lodges of identical design built on a lake's edge, the beach strewn with quartz and granite.

What she was thinking was, Why not make that a wedding venue? She could do that, manage a destination property. It was a fallacy to assume she could only consider jobs in the academy, when there were all these other choices out there, a whole world out there.

The beach would be perfect for an altar, she thought. You would only have to truck in a minimum of sand, and get an archway of twigs, interlaced. The cabins were in good condition, or seemed to be, painted red with a cinderblock foundation. Rudimentary, but that was what people wanted. That was the selling point. Rustic and gritty—but only on the outside. The interiors would be sumptuous. There would be hardwood everywhere, even in the kitchens, vanilla candles provided on check-in, an array of jets in the shower, stones on the floor that massaged your feet as you bathed.

It meant taking on another extensive renovation, true. She would have to be careful not to get in over her head the way she and Dale had with this place. For this reason it would be good to enlist Wayne. This was the exact sort of thing that would interest him. A different kind of challenge than the brewery or converting warehouses into lofts. Money was never the only thing that mattered. He liked risk; he almost never pursued what Sandra would consider straight-ahead investments.

She had nothing else to do today. She could drive to Lighting Works and see if Wayne was there.

And that would be what they served, obviously. Lighting Works and nothing but Lighting Works. Beer and wine. As for food, work with a local caterer, or let people make their own arrangements. Which they would appreciate. From her own wedding she remembered how annoying it had been to be forced to purchase everything on site.

She could live on the property, or close by. Down the road. She would have to be there to attend to the guests, to oversee work that was done in the offseason.

The more she thought about it, the more she realized that Wayne, or anyone else she approached, would have a hard time saying no. It was an obvious win. It couldn't take more than a million dollars of capital. The property was selling for three hundred twenty; she could come in lower than that.

She was typing a note to the realtor when she closed the browser. Abruptly. And got up from her carrel in the library and walked to the elevator. She paced in front of it before sitting on the leather couch that was across from the entrance to the stairwell.

She was leaving, she was betraying him. That was the thought that had crept into her like dread. She could not understand it. Before, staying here and clinging to their old life had seemed like a sentence she had to endure, and Dale would not want that, she was absolutely sure. To say he did not want that was not some romanticization, not one of those backdated requests for permission we so often send to the dead.

Yet when she had started, albeit in this dreamy, torpid sort of way, to contemplate a life without him, it seemed like the worst thing she could do. To him, to anyone. Betrayal. She knew it was crazy, but she found what she wanted to do at the moment was call Dale. Call him up and apologize.

She began spending more time with Tina. Lee gave her a key to the trailer, though often Sandra would pick her up at Chu's, one of Lee's neighbors, who lived on the other side of a shared lawn, next to a volleyball court, now grown over, and a slide and sandbox and swing set. The schedule was patchy. Sandra might watch her for two or three mornings in a row and then go four days without seeing her. She assumed Tina was spending this time with her father, though about him Sandra was not able to glean much, just the usual insults and dismissals from Lee, and from Tina nothing except her dad lived in the jungle place.

"The jungle place," Sandra said. "Who else lives there?"

"Crickets. And bats."

"What do you do when you leave the jungle place?"

"We go bowling."

She stressed the first syllable with relish, and Sandra could see how she enjoyed saying the word.

"Tell me that again. What do you do?"

"We go *bow*ling."

If the weather was clear Sandra would take her to the playground, or the tumble gym that had open hours before the middle school team arrived for practice. At the harbor the big fishing boats came in at three, and they would order donuts and watch the nets tilt and get cantilevered up and be drained of their kill. When it was raining they would stay home and read, or page through the stargazing atlas, and one day Sandra brought her to the colonial mansion that was the heritage museum, to stand in front of the diorama, the scalloped shoreline, with canoes perched on the beach, and they went upstairs and Sandra lifted Tina on top of the old saloon bar, Tina glancing at her reflection in the curved oaken mirror and saying, "Hey Mister," though she could not hold a mean face, could not keep back a grin.

"Now thumb up your hat like this."

Sandra stuck out her lip and pretended to touch the brim of a cowboy hat.

"What's swinging?" she said.

"What's swinging," answered Tina.

In time she discovered Dale. While playing in the upstairs rooms one day, she found a photo album, a holdover from the time when Dale still needed a physical portfolio, and asked whose picture it was in the frontispiece. Sandra said it was Sammy's best friend.

"Where does he live?"

"He used to live right here, in this house."

"Where does he live now?"

"I don't really know," Sandra said. "Some other place. Kind of like a conference. Where you can meet other people and talk to them about what they know that the rest of us don't. Which is quite a lot, by the way. There are things only the people who are there, at the conference, know."

Thereafter it became a game between them. After she told Tina the plan for the day, the girl might suddenly announce that Dale was downtown, or whisper, in mock secrecy, "I think he's going to be there."

"Who?"

"Dale."

"So he's back," Sandra would ask, "back from the conference?"

It was the kind of thing she wanted to tell Dale about. A habit she could not break, even now, close to a month after his death. The conversations she imagined them having were nothing like the ones that occurred a year ago, when he would recoil at any mention of children. The Dale she spoke to now was bemused, eager to talk. If she told him that Tina was smart, he would say, of course, every guardian thinks that.

Guardian. He would use that word, formal, impersonal though it was, to signal that Sandra had more importance and carried more weight in Tina's life than a babysitter. He would know she wanted to hear that.

But if everyone thinks that, and not everyone is smart, then it follows that some people are wrong.

Why yes, yes it does. Thank you for that. May I finish?

Yes. Tell me. I'm sorry. I was just playing. What makes her smart?

Because she has determined, in her four-year-old way, that desire is debatable, desire is up for grabs, whereas need is not. She's found a workaround.

Give me an example.

Okay, so, we're at the café in the bookstore and I order a grape soda. Or not even a soda, just one of those Italian flavored sparkling waters. And Tina realizes that if she says I want that I can say no, that's grown-up water.

So what does she do?

She says, I'm thirsty. Another time when we were standing in front of the glass case she saw a candy pop. Sammy, I'm hungry, she said. Or one day she wanted to wear her tutu but she didn't tell me that. You know what she said? She said it's pink day.

Pink day?

The museum did it once, for a promo, a breast cancer awareness fundraiser, and she got it into her head that it was a regular thing. But you see my point. She doesn't say I want this. She establishes a predicate. Smart.

Yes, it is.

She knows all about you, by the way.

All about me.

Yeah. She says you're at the conference. Or you're back from it.

Conference. Is that code for afterlife?

Not to her. That's the thing. There is no afterlife, no death. In her mind you can appear at any moment, like Elmo or Big Bird.

Pretty exalted company.

She did this and couldn't stop. She knew Dale was dead. She never doubted it for a moment. If she did, there was the urn to look at.

So she had knowledge but not acceptance, or knowledge but not belief. Belief, she decided, must be a rarer, more elusive thing, residing somewhere outside her mind, in the body, or else in some DMZ, a neutral territory, between mind and body, where crucial points were contested. That was what she wanted, what she was striving for, but she did not know how to compel or coerce it.

Beth had said there was a potential buyer, but that Sandra would need to find a certificate of occupancy permit for the porch extension. Something completed before they bought the house, in the earliest stages of restoration, replacing the old porch with one true to the original plans. It should have been handled by the previous owner, she said, but was bound to come up at closing. Sandra was searching through Dale's email, trying to find a letter from the city of Astoria—so far the only note she found was about the sumps in the basement, where to divert that water now that it had been pulled from the sewer line—when Ryan Whitehurst emailed again.

> Hey, wanted to let you know I'll be at Sundance—Stan has an extra pass he can't sell tho I find that hard to believe. Can't remember if you said yr going (I can't find the Bolivian snowboard film on the program)?

Why yes, Sandra wanted to write. I am. Arriving Friday, and I really want to see you. Where are you staying?

Obviously, Dale would not write that. No declarations—that was the rule. Even "I really want to see you" was over the line. The challenge was in finessing it, finding a way to intimate that it would be great to meet, but as the dates didn't match up, no big deal. Sandra moved the cursor to reply. "Hey!" she typed. "Sorry to be writing this late—holidays were brutal, lots of family came out, I tried to lay low but you know how that goes. Can't be done."

That was a lie. She and Dale had debated flying to Louisville at the last minute, to surprise Lucrece, but they stayed home, the first time either had ever done so at Christmas.

> So glad about Mexico—am definitely jealous. And won't be in Sundance, sorry to say. You're going to have to make do without me, though I expect a full report.

You're going to have to make do without me: meaningful, yes, but not obviously so. You could also say it had no significance, and drive yourself crazy trying to decide which.

> I told you about the EPA? Just figuring out if I need to do pickups.

No. She highlighted those sentences and pressed delete. There was no way to know what Dale had told her about the

Environmental Protection Agency. "Still on that EPA gig," she corrected, which put the onus on Ryan Whitehurst to remember what they talked about.

> The last round of notes made me nervous. You'd never expect it, you'd think they'd be laid back, a bunch of granolas, but they're actually pretty cutthroat about stuff.

If it sounded credible that was because it was something Dale had actually said. The first time he described the job, when she asked about the terms of the contract, equipment and frame rate, delivery schedule, and size of the crew allowed.

"They don't know about any of that," he told her. "They're just a bunch of granolas."

She was a little surprised, in truth, at how easy it was to be him, to summon his voice, and without reading the email back she hit Send.

In the morning she checked for a reply and there was none. And no response on the second or third day. Which was not unusual. Almost two weeks had passed between notes from Ryan Whitehurst. Sandra would have to allow for a similar span of time.

She could remember what it was like to get an email from Dale in the days before they were married. She didn't even need to see his name in the inbox. She would get excited before then, at the sight of his initials, the D and T in bold, and while waiting for a message would often be duped by other things she read on her screen.

Designer Tuxedo.

Diamonds Today.

Daytona Track Fire.

She checked Ryan Whitehurst's Instagram. Every time she had done this, she swore it would be the last, yet it was hard to stop—all the vital data was here. Ryan Whitehurst loved candy, frequenting some novelty shop in LA that sold it in barrels, by the fraction of a pound. Gobstoppers and Fun Dip and stuff Sandra didn't know still was made. There were photos of earrings, bracelets with knobs of topaz and other gems. Sandra followed the link—a nonprofit boutique, proceeds going to the families of soldiers killed in Afghanistan. It must be her sister's business, Sandra had concluded. Sister or cousin.

From all appearances Ryan Whitehurst had been on a shoot when Sandra sent the email. The most recent post was of a telephoto lens positioned on the hood of a car. "Settling in for a long one," read the caption, the hashtags #docs and #tryintomakealivingonadayrate and #twerkin.

She felt safe, confident in her anonymity. No one read the *Daily Astorian*, and the alumni magazine had not published a blurb or obituary. As she had never responded to the class secretary, possibly they never would. Googling "Dale Tobin death" led nowhere, only the deaths of other Dales, and a Richard Tobin in Grapevine, Texas. BELOVED BENEFACTOR OF THE COMMUNITY PASSES AFTER LONG BOUT WITH CANCER.

"Mrs. Tobin? Mrs. Tobin."

"Yes. Speaking."

"This is Reverend Samuelson."

"Who?"

"Reverend Samuelson. Your husband—"

"Yes?"

"I was calling to let you know his memorial is finished. In the church."

She let the phone slip from her hand and drifted back asleep. When she woke the digital clock on her nightstand said it was close to noon. It had been a dream, she thought, a test she had failed. Had she been smarter, quicker on the uptake, she might have found a way to ward it off, to stop the news from being delivered.

It wasn't until she was making coffee that she thought of Lucrece's plaque and checked the call history on her phone. She dialed the number back, and when the person answered with the name of the church she could not remember if it was the one where the funeral was held or not.

"Do I need to come and inspect it or anything?" she asked.

"No. I am just letting you know it's there. God bless."

Twice that week she thought she saw him. The first time, in a park with Tina, she did not trust it, and she was right; when she looked away and back no one was there. The next day she was shopping downtown when the skies opened up, the rain tropical in intensity and blowing a stiff onshore wind. She ran with ten or twelve others and took cover beneath the overhang of a department store. And he was there, part of the crowd, craning his head to see around the people and take stock of the storm. She called out to him, she almost hopped up and waved, but by then he was gone.

Examples of magical thinking, she would have called such incidents, and she could see now the door to insanity, the region where grief had stripped all the controls away, and there was nothing to prevent her from walking up to strangers and saying, it's too soon, who are you to comb your hair the way he did, or adopt his mannerisms, the angle of his posture, slightly stooped and round-shouldered?

When she was thirteen or fourteen Sandra had attempted a science experiment. "Notes on Transport" was the title, and it was intended as an etiology of déjà vu. Summer camp gave her the idea, for when she got home after spending three weeks in the mountains she would turn down a corridor, or see the underside of leaves on a tree swaying, and forget where she was, would have to remind herself she was home, and each time she had this sense of déjà vu she logged the time and the circumstance, hoping to identify the precipitating agent, to see if it was a smell or song or a time of day, a shift in the weather, not ruling out the possibility of a force more mysterious, something less visible and subatomic.

Notes on transport. But what happened to her then also happened to her now. Such moments—or not even, fractions of moments—could not be retrieved, not be held onto. As soon as she became aware of them, they were gone.

Dreams were another matter. Dreams alone had the power to draw out the illusion he was still alive, and to wake from them felt like a violation, her eyes slowly compassing the dark. And they left her filled with questions, such as, why did Dale always appear in the same green T-shirt and jeans, and why was he always younger? Not thirty-six, as on the night he died, but some indeterminate age from before they were married. Twenty-eight perhaps. And would it always be like this, she wondered. In twenty or thirty years would she still be dreaming this same version of him?

Because it's not fair, she wanted to say. I need you to come with me. If I'm going to be the one to stay alive, I need you to come with me.

Richard Rawlings said to meet him downtown.

"Now I know that sounds ominous, but there's some stuff you have to sign. Case closed. And good news. I promise. It's good news."

His office was on Exchange Street, not far from Lighting Works and the notions shop that had recently opened. Carmela's Notions Shop. Notions shop, Dale had said, that's another word for thrift store. And he was right. She had visited in the days after Christmas. Prices for the secondhand goods were hard to predict. You could get an antique ironing board for a dollar. A bar stool for ten. But there were also dresses, Victorian types made of crepe and wool, going for four, five hundred dollars. Caps to match. And veils. Such an outfit was in the window now.

She buzzed the intercom and went up to the second floor. There were eight doors, each with the same knocker and eyehole. Richard Rawlings came out of the one on the end to greet her. He was portly, with two dents in his chin, an undefined mass of a backside. When he turned after shaking hands she saw he had missed two loops when putting on his belt.

“So what’s this all about?” she said. “You’ve got me worried.”

He placed a slip of paper on the desk in front of her. A check for more than $50,000 dollars, made out to Sandra Tobin.

“Boom,” he said, in the first display of levity she had ever known him to make.

She picked it up. A cashier’s check, heavier than a personal one, the bottom and top borders perforated.

“Are you serious?” she said.

“Very much so. Look. It’s from Chase.”

“You’re going to tell me there’s some life insurance policy I didn’t know about.”

“No. Those are the missing shares.”

Dale, he explained, had set up a trust, using the cash from the stock sale. He never put it in their account, or the Vestiture account, which is why it did not show up on the statements.

“But I thought it was a charitable donation,” she said. “There’s that form that says it was.”

“He did donate them,” he said. “To his fiscal agent. Higher Plane. So there would be no capital gains. And they sold them and gave him back the money minus four percent. He put some into Vestiture for production and used the rest to pay himself a salary, which I was skeptical about at first but reading the agreement he had with them he was entitled to, up to a certain level. That level was the foundation of the trust.”

He turned a stack of papers around. She picked them up, feeling the heft of the documents, little red notes in the places she had to sign or initial, and flipped her thumb along the edges.

“But this isn’t like—this isn’t some sign that he knew he was going to die? Or not that, because how could he, but just making arrangements.”

“No. I wouldn’t read anything into it. I think he was just worried about the value of the shares over time. Which makes sense. When he sold them they were so high, I or you or anyone would have done the same.”

"Well I guess this means you'll be getting paid," she said after signing, standing and knotting the belt of her coat.

"I guess it does."

She did not cash the check, but put it in the basket by the refrigerator, and told no one about the windfall. Not Cheryl and not Beth. She did not say, here, we can fix the backsplash now, and replace the leaking valve. Her instinct was to wish she had received the money sooner, but on reflection it changed nothing. She would have made the same decisions, would still drive to her parents' house, still try and find some way to finish the dissertation. What it did was make the rest of the year easier. If she found a job or if she didn't, either way now she would not have to worry.

But why did he do it, that's what she wanted to know. There had to be more to it than what Richard Rawlings said. Because if it was only about the values of the shares depreciating, why keep it a secret? Was he preparing for a divorce settlement? If the trust was in her name, if she was, as Richard Rawlings told her, the sole beneficiary, then he had already made his choice, not to contest anything. The stock, the assets. He would give it all to her. The house too probably.

To prove to herself the money changed nothing she submitted her notice, telling the dean she would not be around to teach in the fall, or the summer for that matter. She visited campus for the first time since the accident and found her office had been given to another instructor for the term. When she walked in, he thought she was one of his students. Her personals, the blue books and attendance sheets and letters of rec, were in a closet in the department office. She was about to take them but then decided they would be of no use. She didn't even bother leaving a forwarding address with the department secretary, and when she went in to see the chair she was relieved he did not try to sell her on staying or at least waiting until the summer to say definitively she would not be teaching again. In fact, all he said was, "I can see there's no changing your mind."

He glanced at one of the furnishings on his desk, at a pen cradled like a trophy, made of enamel with golden rings, and she realized she had missed a cue to talk.

"So there isn't then?"

"No."

"Well I guess that's it."

"Not quite," she said. "I want to set up a scholarship in my husband's name. A small one. Maybe it's not a scholarship. Just a stipend to give to a student filmmaker. Preferably one who works with drones. Can you tell me how to do that?"

He said sure, he would have someone from planned giving contact her.

She did tell her parents about the money, the next time they called. In part so they would stop worrying. Between this and the money from the house I will be fine for quite a while, she said. But also—and it was crazy, yet she watched herself doing it even so—she wanted them to be proud of Dale. It made no sense, they had always loved him, their approval had never once shown to be wanting, but here she was, boasting on his behalf. And it wouldn't even be the last time, she saw it was something she would go on doing, for years to come.

"In a decade or two the account would really have accrued," she said. "By my attorney's estimate it would have been two or three hundred thousand dollars."

"So why can't you leave it there?" her father asked.

"That's not how it works."

"What are you going to do with the money?"

"I'm not sure. Hold onto it for now."

Her mother asked what she had done today, and Sandra lied and told her she had gone to a gallery opening even though the event was yesterday and had been virtual. She could have said anything, for she knew her mom was only asking because she had found some new activity for Sandra to do. The beginning of what she said was lost when another call came in. As Sandra did not recognize the number, she did not answer it.

"These are good people, hon."

It was a collective for divorced women. That was what her mom was talking about. Yoga class Saturday morning.

"It's just not good, all that time alone," her mother went on, and Sandra wanted to agree, wanted to say, yes, I know, I'm not trying to become sheltered or be a shut-in, only I don't want to get too good at it too soon. At widowhood. Because it is a skill that I'm improving at, with practice. Practice at hiding displeasure, at suffering other people's kindness, their constant prodding and ministration. If I went to that yoga class, I would be nothing but a foil, something for them to measure their own struggles against, an emblem of the tragedy that lies in wait and can befall at any moment.

"I don't belong there," she said at last. "It's different. Different because Dale and I never got divorced."

"But it's net same, don't you think?"

"No. I don't."

"I mean in twenty years, sweetheart. I'm sorry. It'd be good to meet some of these others. I really think it would—I wouldn't suggest it otherwise."

"Well don't worry. This week I was also invited to basket weaving. Oh, and I was told I could join the country club and have the initiation fee waived."

"Really? How much would that be?"

"Mom."

After she hung up Sandra noticed the number that had called had left a text. It read, "Okay to bring her over? Sorry. Not trying to ambush you. Have just been waiting here and there's no sign and kind of want to get her out of the car."

She was about to write and ask who it was, but she knew there was only one person it could be and she responded by saying, go ahead, you can bring her over, and typed in her address.

From the living room window she watched night settle over the street. After a few moments she got up and put her coat on and had just sat on the stairs in front of the porch when a truck pulled up to the curb. She did not notice it was green until its headlights were off. It was an old model, low to the ground, the paint chipped and the fenders rusty, with bolt-on mirrors clipped to the side. The man who stepped out had the same color hair as Tina, the shade of sandy blond. His cheeks were dimpled, a sandpapery texture, and one of his eyes—the right one—kept blinking, involuntarily, like a spasm. Though he was not unhandsome. She would not have said that.

He introduced himself as Carl Featherstone. There was no backseat in the cab, and he had fashioned Tina's seat using a boat cushion, cutting two slits in the fiberglass base for the seatbelt to pass through.

"Sammy," Tina said, taking her fingers from her mouth.

"Hi sweetheart. Let's go inside." She undid the belt and picked Tina up. When they got in the house she took out some books, but Tina had already gone to work on the couch, turning the cushions sideways to leave just enough room that only she could enter. She named each part of the fort to Carl, then made a tunnel that led to the front window, where she could stand sentry and call out if there were monsters hiding behind the cars parked along the street.

"Looks like she's had some practice with that," Carl said.

"Give me a hand in the kitchen?" Sandra said to Carl.

He followed her through the door and stood by the table in the nook, on which there was nothing but a picture, Dale's wedding picture, in a frame. She could tell he was looking at it even as he did not say anything. She took out the jar of cocoa and the china mugs Tina liked. They had belonged to Lucrece. Painted light blue and yellow, the handle of each had a small depression on it, which Tina called the thumb spot.

"Trays are behind you," she said.

"So you're the nanny?" he said, kneeling down to open the lower cabinet. Not derisively—Sandra could tell he was genuinely puzzled by the arrangement.

"Something like that."

"But you don't have kids."

"No."

"Figured that."

She turned around.

"What does that mean?"

"Nothing. Just that people without kids make the best nannies."

"I would think it would be the opposite."

"I would too."

When he stepped forward to hand her the tray, she smelled something that made her want to stay close to him. A musky, laundered scent, and it was a moment before she realized what it was. His deodorant. Not something she would have ever counted on missing, the smell of a man's deodorant.

"I didn't even know she was with you. I saw her yesterday."

"I was supposed to have her for the weekend. But with Lee sometimes it's best to just not engage. Not take the bait. When she called me up this morning, I didn't even let her get started. I just said okay."

"But what do you tell Tina?" Sandra asked. "She must wonder why her parents are never together at the same time."

"Look here."

On his phone he showed pictures of a house with a garden in the back, a raised wooden walkway winding through native grasses and what looked like two catalpa trees. In some of the photos Tina was crouching, studying a ladybug. The jungle place.

"My sister's husband, he's in the Foreign Service," he said.

"So that's what it is. You're house sitting."

"She don't normally go with him, but this time she did. Tina's got her own room there. Her own floor, as a matter of fact. So I said, Mommy's got to work and Daddy's got to watch Ellen and Mark's house. She gets it."

"But you can't kick the can forever," said Sandra, turning the knob on the stove. "At some point you're going to have to tell her."

“Tell her what? Teenie, your mom’s got to get sober? Teenie, your mom had her chance? Chances. I’ve told her so many times I can’t remember. You really want to hear all this? You got to understand, Teenie shouldn’t even be here. We didn’t know Lee was pregnant.” “We sure as hell weren’t trying. And it had been twenty weeks and she had been drinking some of that and I thought there was no way that child could turn out the way she did and so when Tina was born no problems I said that’s it, we’re not pressing, we’re not going to tempt the house again. This is it.”

He took off his hat and touched his hand to his hair.

“I’ve said that, and I said it would be the last time and then I said it again.”

“Why is she even with Lee then?”

“Tina? That’s on the mediator. We got to go through the process and until we do it’s fifty-fifty. Nothing I can do to change that. My time will come.”

“Meaning what? You are asking for full custody?”

“Expecting to get it too. I just keep a diary, like the mediator said. The phone call this morning, I logged it. Hell, got it down on my phone too, though I’m not sure if that’s—what’s the word? Admissible.”

Sandra poured the water from the kettle into the mugs and stirred the cocoa and set the spoon down and put a bowl of gummy worms on the tray.

“I don’t know about this combination,” he said.

“I don’t either. But it’s her favorite.”

“You going to call her now? Lee.”

“Do you not want me to?”

“It’s a free country. She’ll be here in five minutes, watch.”

“I thought you said she wasn’t at home.”

“I would bet you she is. The whole point is to get me in breach. If she ain’t at home, then there’s no good option. Right? I can’t take her back to Portland with me and I can’t leave her with you. Either way I’ll be making a wrong move. Everything she does is for the fight. That’s the thing with Lee. The fight is all.”

"Well you better skedaddle then," Sandra said. "But let me ask you something: do you make telescopes?"

"Do I what?" he said, the eye blinking again.

"Make telescopes."

"Sort of. I suppose at one time you might say I had a hand in it. FLIR up at Wilsonville, where I was, they make the infrared on some of NASA's stuff. So I got to show Tina some pretty cool things."

"Cool things."

"Star clusters—deep space. Readouts and maps and such. There was a portal on their website and we used to scan through."

She waited in the kitchen while he said goodbye to Tina, and when he was gone, she gave him fifteen minutes of lead time before sending a text to Lee. There was no answer. Sandra warmed up some chicken and read a book to Tina, and this time she called but there was still no answer from Lee. She told Tina they were going home. It was past ten, and by the time they pulled into Butte Farms Tina had fallen asleep, the fingers slipping from her mouth. Sandra brought her inside and laid her on the bed—there was only one, a queen, which she guessed meant Lee and Tina both slept there—and searched through the drawers until she found some pull-ups and changed her and then pulled the blanket up and turned out the light.

From the living room she crossed to the sink, the floor's linoleum buckling beneath her, and turned on the tap to get a glass of water. On the counter was a stack of dishes and a coffee filter full of grounds. For some reason she thought the room smelled of a cat's litter, though there was no sign of a pet. Behind a mason jar with a few green buds sprouting out of a cake of dirt she found a sheaf of Tina's drawings, some loops done in crayon and a series of outsized, crooked letters, and she took the folder to the couch and sifted through it, wondering when Tina had made these and where, if drawing was something Lee did with her at home or if in the months before Sandra knew her she had gone to classes at day care.

If Lee was not back by one o'clock, she decided—only she was incapable of finishing the thought. At one o'clock there was nothing she could do. She couldn't go out and look for her, couldn't leave Tina alone. For a moment she considered bringing her to Chu's, but when she looked through the window she saw the lights of her trailer were off. Besides which her interactions with Chu had been brief, and she had a newborn and another child, three years old. There was no going over there. The only thing was to wait and drive Tina back to Portland in the morning.

"Okay to bring her over?" was what Carl had written when she was on the phone with her parents.

"Can I drop her off with you first thing in the a.m.?" she typed into the thread, and decided to add, in case it wasn't clear, "I took her home, but Lee's still not here."

She checked on Tina and spent several minutes trying to find the thermostat. That she could not almost threw her into a panic until she realized the baseboards were controlled individually. She went around checking each one, putting her hand over it to make sure it was warm. She tried watching television but was too distracted and turned back to the folder of Tina's drawings. It was only when she heard a siren that she realized she had fallen asleep, for five minutes, and when her phone lit up she thought it was Carl but the message was from Lee, saying she would be right over. Sandra went outside. The street was quiet. She could hear the cones around the electrical lines buzzing, and she waited for the lights of a taxi or Lee's car but then saw a figure on the edge of the road trip and get up and wipe their hands across their pants. She turned and flipped on the outer light and stood in the door before Lee had a chance to open it.

"Lee, what the fuck is this?" she said, twisting her arm so Lee could get a look at her watch. "It's midnight. More than that. It's almost one."

Lee tried to go through the door, but Sandra blocked the way. She was wearing the hoodie, jeans, and flip-flops, though it was not fifty degrees outside.

"Carl tried to bring her back. And you weren't home."

"I know," Lee said.

"What do you mean you know?"

"It was what he wanted. He planned it all along. The fucking asshole."

Sandra stepped out onto the cinderblock and pulled the door shut. Now she could smell the alcohol on Lee, on her clothes and breath.

"What are you talking about?"

"He's trying to steal her from me."

"Shut up. Stop. Just stop, okay? Tell me why you weren't at home."

"Yeah, see, you're not going to believe me either. Your mind is made up. But it ain't his day to watch her, and when I called and told him he better watch himself he suggested bringing her over to your house. Called it the neutral party. Said he preferred it. Keep it nice and easy. The fucking coward. He didn't even want to see me."

"What were you going to do, let her stay with me the whole time?"

"He can't just be doing any old thing he pleases, making up the rules as he goes along. He'll have to learn. And he will, won't he?"

The next day Lee sent a text thanking Sandra for bringing Tina back the night before.

"It's all of us now who have to put up with his bullshit," she wrote.

Sandra did not know what to believe, if it was true that Carl planned to drop Tina off at her house all along, or which one of them Tina was supposed to spend the day with. It didn't matter. She had to get out, had to stop seeing Tina, for the simple reason that compacts were not made with a person like Lee. The constant outpouring of grievance, and the quicksilver changes, the about-faces from truculence and scorn to its opposite: once enmeshed in that you could never gain a footing, and she had been deceiving herself if she thought she could help Tina, and perhaps Lee, when it was clear the whole tragic course was set and she was powerless to do anything about it. Worse than powerless. She was going along for the ride.

Say goodbye now, she told herself. Today. Tina had already seen some of the boxes. It wouldn't be too hard, explaining it to her.

But she couldn't do it—couldn't turn away. Not because of how it looked on the outside, to a person like Cheryl, who would assume she was clinging to Tina because she and Dale were never able to start a family. That was the obvious reading. A surrogate child, a proxy. Or more: a substitute for Dale. Lose one presence, gain another.

And maybe that was true. Maybe Tina was a proxy for what she wanted with Dale. A stand-in. Fine. But it was more than that, and Sandra knew it was something she would never tell another person but would become one more forgotten utterance, part of the legion of things we say to ourselves and never to other people.

What was it? This: her time with Tina was totally absorptive. She could concentrate on something else. On her. Not that she was unaware of Dale's death, but she was able to see around it, for a minute or seconds at a time. It was still there but hazy, indistinct, a shelf of cloud. And one can live like that, she thought, under a shelf of cloud. Without any of the usual exhaustion or pressure in the chest. Just this faint dull hurt along the edges.

From the beginning she had understood grief to be a vigil. You are waiting for something but don't know what. And perhaps Tina was showing her the terms, the best life could offer, in that Dale's death would retreat, not all the way, no—of course not—but now and then, to make room for something else.

The dealmaker, that was how Sandra thought of her. That was who she was.

When Ryan Whitehurst wrote back this is what she said:

> Hey, no worries, I totally understand. Holidays are crazy. Survival really is the only goal. At Christmas I was at my mother's place with like forty others. That side of the family is brutal and I just kept wandering off to the bathroom with my phone. And the

whole question was, how much time in here is permissible? When will they start to notice I'm gone?

Sundance was great. I know yr supposed to bitch about it but it was an amazing couple of days. You should definitely go.

Sandra wrote,

Bitch about it why, because it's too corporate? I hate that, the way you're not allowed to enjoy anything anymore. What did you see?

The reply this time was immediate. Not even twenty-four hours.

Yeah, that's the line, that it's gotten too big for its britches and is just a place for heavy hitters, not independents, in other words the very thing it was designed to thwart. I didn't see anything you would call spectacular. On the last day I rented skis and made a complete ass of myself on the bunny hill before waving the white flag and going into the lodge. I ended up getting pretty wasted and came down with a cold and am only now emerging from a hideous chrysalis of mucus.

Sorry to hear that, hope you're feeling better. Did you take time off?

No, had to work straight through. It's crazy town around here. We're filming Neil Young on Wednesday.

For real?? Is he going to play?

No. I would have loved that, but we were only given thirty minutes and it was a hard out. One of his managers did a film back in the 80s and Stan was one of the producers on that and that's really the only reason it happened. But he was cool, he answered four questions but didn't autopilot them and was really funny. He gave a shit.

Good. You hear so many horror stories you start to assume the worst about people, though maybe you're not one of those Neil was a dick you couldn't put his records on after. That was Mel. All the times he was awful I would say, hey, there's nothing in the contract that says he has to be nice. It's a bonus if that happens but the work stands on its own, I mean isn't that the point?

You never said Mel was bad. I feel like there are some horror stories yr not sharing with me.

He could unload on a whim, someone he had never met and who wasn't in charge of decisions anyway, and also be mean to those who were trying to help. Friends at Warners, the curator of the museum here. He didn't seem to realize they were on his side.

What was that Neil shoot for, anyway?

Not telling. Remember the Ryan Whitehurst rule!

Wait, I do sort of, but can you explain it to me again? Sorry!

The only time to be worried about something is when it's a no-brainer. That's the rule. Originally I came up with it for film but more and more I think it applies to life in general. Nothing scares gatekeepers in this town like a sure-fire winner. If you have a great idea, that's the biggest red flag. Not that this was my idea but you know what I'm saying. But it's all good now. I think this series is about to get the green light, a sort of history of bootleg records and their effect on the music industry, so we can talk about it. Stan has some champagne and we're all going to pop it later. Watch this and obviously don't share. The password is gobetween.

She watched the reel while sitting at the tumble gym one day. Tina was on the other side of the mat, using a foam pedestal to hang from the rings and bars. It began with a close-up of a record being placed on a turntable. That shot dissolved into an eight-track and a cassette, a CD, and finally a laptop with the words "Atlas Productions Presents the Secret History of the Recording Industry" on the screen. Disembodied sound bites, voices talking over footage of Bob Dylan and Sinatra.

"His unreleased stuff? If you haven't heard that"; she hit pause before the sentence was over.

It was not bad. But it was not good, either. Every music documentary Sandra had ever seen—and every sizzle reel for a documentary, for that matter—started this way. With the summary, the broad outline, and lots of declamation, the interview subjects offering blurbs for the movie they were about to appear in.

Dale would notice none of this. He would be focused on the lighting and patterns in the background, alert to any errors or shortcuts taken in the visual approach. Story structure, for him, was a subordinate concern. Wizardry or sleight of hand tacked on only after the real problems of production had been settled.

But what did any of this matter, she thought. The reel was not the point. The point was to figure out what happened between them, and she could not lose her way, not lose focus, until she had used the correspondence to wrest some confession from Ryan Whitehurst.

And then she would know. For better or worse she would know.

She tried to write some notes that would steer the conversation toward Seattle. More and more she was convinced that if something had happened it was in Seattle, last July, when they attended the same conference. Dale had gone to inspect some equipment by Boeing. Ryan Whitehurst and the rest of the Atlas team were there as coproducers of a virtual reality film that was being screened.

She could imagine the two of them at the bar, sitting on a couch or chaise, grateful for any interruption, for a line producer or programmer to wander in, someone vaguely known and whose leaving would restore them to each other, sharpening the sense of isolation and time stolen. Two hours and one of them saying, okay, I have to go to bed, then riding the elevator together, the door opening and their rooms not on the same floor so the pause, the moment of indecision, before one fell into the other.

Nothing could be easier, Sandra thought. Nothing in the world.

On his credit card statement she found an entry for the bar tab. At least she thought she did. A room charge labeled food and drink, for eighteen dollars. What did this mean, that he had one drink, a bourbon or martini, and called it a night? Had one drink and went upstairs with her? Or paid for the subsequent rounds with cash?

> So, I don't think I told you this, but I have to go to Seattle again. A long story with a terrible client. I'll explain later. What was the name of that place we ended up?

> Got up last night at like three o'clock, and for the briefest of moments I was so happy, refreshed, and could not understand why. And then when I was looking out the bathroom window I realized it was because I had a dream about you, about us.

> It makes me think of that night in Seattle. Do you remember?

Of course, none of these drafts worked. They were too trashy, unctuous, or bald. Too on the nose. Like writing, "I really want to see you." There was no artistry in it. There had to be suggestion first, the whole point was to send it in code, circumspectly, or risk it falling apart. As if the feeling and style of expression were inseparable, and to swap out one would do irrevocable harm to the other.

She would have to be patient, then, and move within the constraints of the genre. And not be so terse. That was the thing about the notes she had written so far. She would have to give a little, not withhold quite so much, while remaining vigilant, on the watch for a time when she could move in confidently and make everything known. She thought of chess players, the grand masters, who plot eight or twelve moves ahead.

Hi Ryan, it's very good, and congratulations on the series getting picked up. I love the lighting on the guy who's down in his basement and there's nothing on his shelves except vinyl. It looks like a bomb shelter and the only thing he cared to move down there were his records.

So is this it, tracks from the bootlegs and interviews with songwriters about what it's like to lose control of their catalog? I can see where it goes, they embrace the concept and make millions, right? The stars follow the fans. The fans are leaders, the process flows the other way.

Yeah, it's his whole apartment, shelves, he's got like two thousand and he wasn't even the craziest one we interviewed. Stan found all these collectors, plus the people who make the bootlegs, and it's a whole other subculture I never knew about, like baseball cards or video games. And that's what the series is really about. I mean, yeah, there will be a comprehensive sweep about how bootlegs evolved from this homemade thing and became a powerful competitor but to be honest the premise is really devotion, mania, how people become stuck on a song or artist and can't get enough of it.

And I suppose they're all male, yes? Sorry, not trying to reduce—being serious. Because there's all this research about men shading more on the autism spectrum.

Yeah, I guess yr right. I never thought of that. They are male. Every one of them. I'll have to mention that to Stan. But it's a problem if they come off as freaks. I sort of admire it. What they do, what they're invested in. All my addictions are unhealthy I feel like.

So, can't let you get away with saying your addictions are unhealthy and not following up.

Oh, it's nothing scandalous or sexy or even all that interesting. Sorry to disappoint. I've gone on like twelve social media cleanses, with varying degrees of success. Eight days I think is my record. One thing I did kick was Trump's Twitter. I would check it all the time, at the office, watching dailies, it was a total addiction. I would get depressed if he went off to visit some foreign head of state and couldn't be counted on to tweet some dumb shit at his regular time.

Wait, you were addicted to it because of how stupid he was? I sort of get that. It was like a class in dramatic irony, that feed. My favorite was when he would tweet out something solemn and respectful in the midst of a tirade. I remember one, it was like Holocaust Remembrance Day, he sent out this photo of him and Melania kneeling in front of some wreathes or candles, the caption "never forget" and three minutes on either side was a bunch of insane stuff about presidential harassment or one of his former cabinet members.

I keep waiting for the bracket, for someone like Colbert to do a contest of the greatest, and by that I mean craziest, tweets. Make it like the basketball tournament, Trump Madness, you whittle it down to 32 of the most infamous tweets, hamberder and Prince of Whales and stone cold loser and husband from hell and the audience votes on what is the most batshit.

And now that we're talking about it it makes me want to check his account. And I can't. It's a zero-sum game. Nothing ever matters. I kept waiting for an aha! or fall from grace but one half reacts, one half says the other half overreacts. Repeat. Every four days, repeat. And the whole time I knew it was unhealthy. I wouldn't even log in under my account but would check on an incognito tab so it didn't show up in my history.

Ever wonder what people did for obsession back in the day? Before social media I mean. Where were the rabbit holes? The public library?

Yeah, maybe. The newspaper. Who knows. How about you? What are the rabbit holes?

Oh, Zillow is a particular weakness. Hours a day on the app. I guess you can justify it because I'm selling the house and need to find something but I also look at places all over, places I can't afford. It is hard to stop.

Wait, yr selling yr house? When did you decide this?

During New Year's. Astoria has sort of run its race in my opinion.

So yr not just moving, yr moving . . . but haven't made up your mind? Tell me more! Obviously I cast my vote for LA.

I have no idea. And I'm not just saying that to be evasive. At first I thought I would go to Portland, then I was like, I'm not even from Oregon, why do I have to stay here? Or Seattle, a lot of people here end up there or vice versa. Then it's like you're moving in stages. First you go a little ways, then farther, then farther still . . .

Well, glad to hear it, I don't like the thought of you living in Portland. It's such a cliché, don't hate me, but I don't think I could handle the rainy season. Such an LA girl!

Yeah. But you know, this time of year is not even the worst. The worst is April or May, when it seems like the whole rest of the country is experiencing spring and you're in the dreariest spot imaginable. You totally lose your mind.

I made a list. I won't tell you which cities were on it but I was going to be like the Wall Street firm that picks stocks each year by throwing darts. Just toss it and see where it lands. But seriously, there's no rush. It's such an important decision, I'm just going to get out of here and stay with my parents for a while and see what turns up. Sort of starting over. Not to mention I have my hands full trying to unload this thing. It's more work than you can imagine, repairs and foundation reports.

Okay, wow. I'm not even sure how to handle this news or what to say. Good luck with everything? And tell me why there's so much work or repairs.

So it's old. That's the first thing. The deed I think says 1905, which means it has some nice features, the wood on the doorframes is cypress, which they don't use anymore, and never did except in these old Victorian homes. Where it was a staple.

It's weird how you can live somewhere and only glimpse the history behind it. This neighborhood is like a mecca for googie enthusiasts, which I didn't even know about until one day I saw a tour bus and then later someone said it's the last weekend to see this carhop because they're tearing it down.

Yeah, that's it. The architect of this house is some legendary figure, they teach him, or some of his work, in schools and there's even a society in England devoted to him. I know because the realtor does a lot of work with them and it was one of the first places she reached out to seeing if they wanted to buy it.

Sounds fancy, I know, but it's really a tomb. The previous owner bought it with the intention of restoring it. That was his thing, gobble up properties and redo and price them out. When the crash hit he was left holding the bag on like ten. This is one.

Wow, I had no idea—you never told me you were living in a work-in-progress. Did you ever get into that show Fixer Upper? I watched the whole thing, every episode, and couldn't figure out why except I'm terrible at it. Repairs. I don't even go to IKEA for stuff because you have to put it together. I find things already assembled and have TaskRabbit bring it over.

When we bought it we said that's part of the fun, having this project to keep us busy on weekends and whatnot, but it didn't turn out that way. Though it's what allowed us to get this place for a song. The third floor was basically carpet bombed and we had to redo all the walls. But as soon as you think you're done you realize you're not. The goalposts are always changing. Finish the upstairs, no, get a permit for the porch extension. Get that and hold on, there's something with the subfloor, and on and on.

When's the air date for the first bootleg episode by the way?

December, which means we've got to be locked late August and start editing as soon as possible. The shooting schedule is bananas. San Francisco, New York, Stan wants to get B-roll of the shops, though I think there's only one left, Generation on Thompson, that stills sells bootlegs like they used to. One collector lives in east Texas.

Are you still on the EPA thing? You always keep me in the dark about everything.

No, the EPA thing is in a holding pattern. I don't know what the plan is. I could be done, could be at the halfway point, who knows. They sent a check on the first of the month but I haven't touched the cut in weeks.

Didn't you tell me last year about some doc on Dolly the sheep?

Close. Dolly is in it, but it's really about this team of researchers, headed by a Nobel Prize winner, trying to figure out a way to use genetically modified pig organs for transplants. A good story but it fell through. The filmmakers lost funding. The production budget was a write-off for some pharmaceutical giant whose shares cratered.

So if I'm reading this right, then yr getting paid now not to work? Kind of hating you right now. I want that job. That's one post I don't care if it's filled or not. But seriously I fucked up, because if I knew you were free I would totally have asked you to DP on some of these bootleg shoots. Stan brings his own guys, natch, but I would have made the hard sell. This weekend even—what are you doing this weekend? Can I convince you to come to L.A.?

Why, do you want to meet somewhere? I could do that. Would have to look at flights though. Flights and a hotel.

No, we don't have the budget, we went with somebody local. It was for a commercial. You could have done it in your sleep, I almost feel sorry asking. Two FS7.

Well, thanks for thinking of me. And I'm not particular about jobs, just so you know. Work is work.

That's a good attitude to have, if yr free and on yr own . . . I really think if you came down here you could do as much or as little as you like. Phone would be ringing off the hook.

I appreciate that. What was that commercial for anyway?

A foundation for research into finding a cure for Wilms Tumor. Someone on their board sits on the board for Chevron. We did something for them last year. A promo for one of their junkets. And when I was talking to this exec about it I learned this charity is like his baby. I had a brother die from Wilms Tumor, so when he mentioned it I told Stan we were doing this free of charge no questions asked. So you get it, right? If we're doing this commercial pro bono and I told him we're flying in a DP he would have lost his shit.

Ryan, I'm sorry to hear that. About your brother. Tell me how long ago was that.

When I was little. He was getting treated and everything looked like it was getting better and then he fell unconscious in the stroller and that was it. I was four but it gets twisted in my mind, I may not be remembering the death but hearing about it later, from my parents. His birthday is September 16 and I still fly home for it. I only missed one time, the semester I studied abroad. And it's not a sad day. We don't do anything special. We're just together is all.

I'm glad you do that. It's important. You have to do those gestures. It's what keeps people with us. And that's hard to do.

It is hard. I just worry, I don't know if this is making sense, I just worry that if you don't talk about it then you train yourself not to think about it. Not to remember. And I still think of him, even in the weirdest situations, if I just hear the name Larry, his name was Lawrence, he didn't live long enough for people to call him Larry but I still think of him if I hear it—I worry that I'm flinching somehow, trying to block it out.

That seems like a natural fear to have, though I would say if you're conscious of it that's a good first step, like you're processing it. Why don't you like to talk about your brother, because it's such a private thing?

Yeah, and some reactions are not the best. Give any indication yr still thinking about it, the person might think there is something wrong with you, like yr dwelling on it or obsessed, and I always want to be like, hey, what's the statute of limitations on grief? Because I didn't know there was one.

Also, and I hope I don't sound like an ass here, but you do hear the dumbest shit. The worst clichés. Time heals all wounds.

That's a classic. He's in a better place now.

Everything happens for a reason.

The Lord works in mysterious ways.

The only way out is through. People say all this, they don't mean you. They mean them. It's for their benefit. They're tired of worrying about you, they've felt the sting of sympathy long enough. So they say you need to get closure or you have it or you need to find it or you will one day and then they've done their part. They can bow out. But I think even then they know it's a falsity. I think about how Lawrence's death changed my parents, it's not like there can be any end of it.

Wait, so how did it change them? Not trying to dwell on this. You don't have to answer if you don't want.

So obviously I'm not a shrink or a therapist, so take this at face value, but as best as I can tell—and yr like the only person I've said this to—it just cut their ability to respond to anything. Like there were no surprises anymore. The other shoe had dropped. They had nothing to fear or work to avoid. Which sounds great, but it's not like they went to Vegas and let it ride or became real estate speculators. They just went into their shell. They couldn't be stunned or excited anymore. It made me sad to see.

Thank you. I understand. I mean, I don't, I know that's insulting, I'm just saying what you said makes sense to me. Whatever. The reason I asked was because someone I know and was really close to died on New Year's Eve.

Oh, I'm so sorry to hear that Dale!! What happened?

We were at this party and he left and was driving on the bridge that crosses into Washington and a flatbed floated over from the opposite lane and pinned him to the wall. I don't know for certain and don't think I want to know but it was over right away. The glass was blown out of the car and it almost spilled into the river.

OMG, is there anything I can do? Was the driver drunk?

No. That's what's crazy, the reason he died was to avoid drunk driving. We were at a party getting ready to leave and go to this brewery and one of our friends called and said his DD bailed and he wasn't going to make it. So this person, the man who died, said okay, I'll drive over. The friend, Anderson, lives way up in Ilwaco and the Ubers at this time on New Year's were way over a hundred dollars. So he said, I'm going. I was like, what for, we're already late. And he said, big deal, it's just a New Year's Eve party. But it was our friends who were hosting and we continued to argue about it and he said it won't even be an hour and that was it. I never saw him again. I saw his taillights make the turn and followed him down one more street and he was dead a few minutes later.

Dale I had no idea you were dealing with this. It's terrible. Is the driver of the truck going to jail?

Yes. He pled guilty to a manslaughter charge and is going to serve some time but I don't know how much. I stopped following it. There's really no point. It just eats you up and he's not coming back. The driver testified, or his lawyer in an affidavit said, he had a case of apnea that was undiagnosed and had fallen asleep, maybe, maybe not, I guess we'll never know. As I said, that's not the stuff I try to focus on.

So what do you focus on? If you don't mind me asking.

I focus on not focusing.

I get that. And sorry to be late in writing. No special reason. Just work. We had to show the first assembly of the bootleg project.

I've let all my other pen pals go, if it makes you feel any better.

And same deal with you as with me, okay? I'm here to talk about it if you want. Or not. We never have to. It's up to you.

Thank you. Leaving here will be important. Though I hate saying I'm going to start a new life. Because there's no such thing, right? I try not to say it.

Wait, what are you talking about, the reason why yr moving or the person who died or both? I don't think moving away is a violation of loyalty. It doesn't have to be an either-or.

You're right. It's not. And did I tell you I got an offer. Three. So it's vaya con dios. And I have to give my realtor credit, I didn't want to wait, I wanted to jump at the first one, but we had a deal, she and I—she didn't want me to sell the house as is, she wanted to dump all this money in and wait a year and get a lot of media attached—and I said no, and she said, well, how about this, if the opening offer doesn't meet a certain figure then I have to wait ten days, and she was right, in ten days we got two more bids and I took the last one.

Congratulations. That's a weird thing to say. Is it the right thing? And does this mean yr homeless now?

Pretty much. I mean, I'm not, I'm still here, but officially, yes, legally yes. Homeless. Just have to pack it all up. And figure out which furniture to unload and what to save. God is it tedious.

Wait, yr still there?

Dear Ryan, thank you for the gift. It's very nice of you. The card is beautiful and I laughed when I saw the key ring—it was just what I needed. It's on my desk now, or the box I'm using as a desk. Is it an heirloom? You'll have to fill me in on it sometime.

Yr funny. I hope you haven't forgotten what it is. Or his name! I actually saw his name in another setting, a serious setting, not too long ago and couldn't find a way to tell people why I was laughing, I wasn't trying to be rude.

I wasn't sure who was getting mail at that address so I made it out to Vestiture because you can never be too careful.

Right. I appreciate the precautions.

So if the house is sold and you don't need to be there I assume yr free next weekend. We're going to be in the Bay, shooting the Fillmore.

It's not the original Fillmore is it? I get these venues confused, especially when they put an old name on someplace new. I feel like you're going to ask me to shoot again. Thank you. Though you know I can't.

No, it's the same, or at least it's the same address. Stan wants us to grab B-roll of the place, there's this whole thread in the movie about the Dead and how they were ahead of their time with the taping culture. But I was asking because after we wrap I could drive somewhere. Not saying you'd have to come all the way down. I was even thinking the Redwoods until I looked at a map and saw they weren't halfway, or close. But I like the idea—have you ever been? Flights to Eureka are cheap so after I turn in the equipment I could head to SFO. Will you have yr car?

I'm not sure. To pick you up at the airport? Where are you staying?

Actually, scratch that, I was wrong, the second flight that day is sold out and when I said they were cheap I was looking at the early one. I'm on that and I'll just go ahead and rent a car since it'll be morning when I get in.

I did a little research and this place seems like it's not too horrible an option. On the site it said they only had two rooms for the weekend so I went ahead and nabbed one. No pressure, okay? If you want to show up, you can. If yr ready. If not then you know I will understand.

Sandra was surprised at the modesty of the place Ryan Whitehurst had chosen. The Lost Whale Inn. A plain house with four dormers and metal siding, situated on a hill over a cove, the Redwoods stretching in all directions. There were eight rooms. She scanned the pictures of each and considered her options.

She could send a letter to the front desk.

Dale is dead, I am his wife, I found your emails.

I am sorry but I cannot be here. I changed my mind. I never loved you.

Yet it would be better, would it not, to confront her, to go and watch the shock spill across Ryan Whitehurst's face, and the fumbling, vain attempt at apology? She might deny it, even there. Invent an alibi on the spot. But it wouldn't matter. She would know—for the rest of her life she would know—that Sandra had found out the truth.

She could also kill her. Seriously. For why bother with half measures, when she could let her check in, do a quick inventory of the room, then follow her into the woods and use a knife, antifreeze on a dishrag, something.

Only she couldn't be the one to do it. The more Sandra thought about it the more she realized she wouldn't be able to plunge the knife in or thrust her knees into the small of Ryan Whitehurst's back, to make sure she didn't wrestle free before suffocating. She would have to find someone. Drive up to the Column and act like she was looking to buy pot or heroin and after the arrangements were made flee for Venezuela or Belize or some other nation without an extradition treaty. Where the dollar was like gold, where she would still have enough money left, even after the murderer's ransom.

But of course the only option was to do nothing. It was over. The correspondence had done its job. She would have preferred to find out without giving away quite as much of herself as she had, but at least she knew. Ryan Whitehurst had invited him to stay with her in the Redwoods, at a bed and breakfast. This was as close to proof as she was ever going to get.

She deleted Dale's email account. Ryan Whitehurst would not write again, she was confident of that. It was one of the rules of affairs. Or one of the rules of affairs as Sandra imagined them. After all the risk involved in making arrangements—the energy a person would have to expend working themselves up to propose or accept an offer—there would come a lull, an interval of silence, lest any word incite second thoughts, a cowering or retreat.

And anyway she had hedged, Sandra thought, remembering the last email. They never made plans. Not officially. All Ryan Whitehurst said was I'm going, if you want to show up you can.

So Sandra didn't have to do anything. She did not have to answer.

She exported his tax documents, a few files Richard Rawlings had told her to save, and forwarded some pictures to her own account. She was expecting more security questions, a secondary form of validation, be it a code sent to a phone or another email address, but she had only to enter the password, and she typed in Brooklyn10 and the page collapsed into the welcome screen.

She did not tell Lee she was moving, for she did not trust her to relay the news to Tina in a fair or even way. She did mention it to Carl, sending a text to say this was going to be her last week in Astoria. "Just FYI," she wrote.

In the meantime, Tina wanted to know why Sandra was sending her home with some toys after each visit. A plastic triceratops, crayons worn down to the nub. Sandra said, "Sammy's taking a trip. Going away for a bit, but we'll do something special on my last day, okay? I'll find out what. I'll make the plans."

"Are you going to the conference?" Tina asked.

Closing was in thirty days—shorter than normal, Beth explained, since there would be none of the negotiations and handwringing that usually accompany a sale.

"'As is' is nice that way," she said.

"So I don't have to be here."

No, Beth said, but she did have to authorize someone to appear in her place to make all the signatures.

"Do you know an attorney?"

"I do," Sandra said. "But the sign's still out front."

"We just do that in case," said Beth. "You don't have anything to worry about. This is a lock."

There were ten days before the Lost Whale Inn. Packing would take at least half that span, and there was the inspection to supervise, though Beth had told her not to worry about it, that it was mostly for the city's records, the updating of permits.

She pulled up the map. It was almost two thousand miles to her parents' place. Out to Spokane, through towns she had never heard of, like Cle Elum, Moses Lake, and Yakima, then across the Bitterroots. At Billings the route forked, and she could go south, over the Badlands, or stay on 90 and traverse the prairie of North Dakota. A shorter way, though she would have to contend, at this time of year, with snow and black ice.

On the day of the appointed rendezvous, then, she would be gone. By the time Ryan Whitehurst checked into the Lost Whale Inn, Sandra figured to be somewhere around Miles City, Montana.

She was going to rent a storage unit, but prices were too high. Now that she had come into money she did not want to spend it on moving expenses. Or be bound to Astoria. If she ever came back, she wanted it to be of her own choosing, not because she was checking on stuff or picking up stuff. Moving companies also were expensive, and there was no address to give them. She had no idea how long she would stay with her parents or where she would go next.

Renting a van was out of the question once she took a test drive and saw how uncomfortable the lack of a rearview mirror made her. She could not drive halfway across the country without being able to see behind her.

So she would take the things herself, and anything that did not fit in the car would be given away. She was anticipating great difficulty in this, but she began to make three or four trips to Goodwill in the afternoon. Some of the stuff Lucrece had marked for giveaway was still in boxes. Glancing at things she had sworn, months ago, never to get rid of, Sandra recalled the first days after the accident, the fatigue and soreness, how every touch was blunted, as though she had been filled with nitrate or some other benumbing substance.

For this reason they were easy to part with, Dale's sweaters and books and the file folders full of receipts. Truthfully she did not want to see most of it again.

Beth found a secondhand dealer in Manzanita who would buy most of the furniture and pick it up after she was gone. The bedroom set and couch, the bureau in the living room. Dale's equipment, his drones and dolly and cables, she donated to Clatsop, though she knew she ought to sell it. There was money to be made, a few thousand dollars, but then she would have to research the items, describe and vouch for their condition, negotiate the offers, and that could take weeks. She removed the luggage tag from one of the cases—Dale's New York address was still written on it—and tore off a sticker that was from some trip when he had passed through customs.

Sam Varner himself came in the grip truck to take it away. "I heard you were leaving," he said after she helped him load the heaviest case, a tortoiseshell box with lenses inside, packaged in foam, and something in her was moved to bring up the night she had gone to Lighting Works and tried to meet up with him.

"You know I texted you the other night," she said, before realizing it was not the other night, but several weeks ago. "Or tried to. I had the wrong number."

"What was it about," he said, "all this stuff?"

"No. Something else."

Taking pictures down from the wall, the wedding portraits, a facsimile of one of the earliest charts of Astoria's harbor, with primitive depth measurements—spirals to mark a shallow or sandbar—she found pencil marks on the walls, a series of dots and hatchings. Some buried cuneiform she could not decipher. But when she dismantled the table in the guest room she saw the same pattern, and recognized the dots as Dale's. It was the looping eye or curlicue with which he closed each shape that tipped her.

She filled a bucket with soap and water and tried to scrub the markings off. They would not erase. She left the sponge in the bucket and tried one of the tin brushes in the sink. No use. They seemed permanent, as if they had been made with eyeliner or a graphic designer's pencil.

He was going to make bookcases. That's what it was. And had marked off the space and, she remembered now, even gone to the lumberyard. He found the boards online, flanges made of teak, and drove to inspect them.

And then what? What had happened to this plan, to all their plans? On their honeymoon they sat at the bar and on a napkin wrote down a bucket list, though that was not what Dale called it. He called it a program of action. She laughed at him, but he said, Seriously. Dying, we'll get to that later.

Getting their scuba license. Climbing the forty-six peaks of the Adirondacks. Paying for and serving Thanksgiving dinner at a food shelter.

Now she thought it was perfectly named. A program of action.

Anything could go on it, Dale said. Anything we can do together, that is, not singly. That was the requirement.

She searched everywhere for the napkin. She spent all of one day, looking in the file cabinets in Dale's office, emptying the drawers of her rolltop desk. She opened books consigned for giveaway.

It never turned up, but what she did find, in one of the copy boxes Dale kept behind his desk, stacked to form a pedestal on which he would fix things or read things, was a computer printout. Fax instructions from the investment firm that handled the conversion of stock. Clipped below it was a section from her dissertation, from chapter five, with a number at the bottom, 244, representing the number of words on the page. The date September. Not long after Labor Day.

And then she realized she had been wrong when she told Richard Rawlings Dale never said anything about the trust. It was not in July, when Richard Rawlings said the shares were wiped from his statement. It was here, at the end of summer. She had completed a draft—that was why he put her on the word quota, so she could be done, or almost done, by the start of fall term—but she told him not to get carried away. To temper his congratulations.

"Because it's still going to be another year," she said. "A year at least. Assuming the defense goes well I'm still going to have to wait for the job market to open up."

"So is that what you want to do?" he asked, and she had seized on the word.

"Want?" she said. "Don't you think *want* is a luxury?"

An evasion, because what she really wanted to say but did not have the courage to, was, what have I been spending all this time on, the last five years, if it wasn't to apply for academic jobs?

If her younger self had heard that, heard her say want is a luxury, she would have cringed, and considered the remark—and rightly, Sandra believed—a sign of weakness. The whole reason she had turned to ichnology to begin with was because she wanted to do it. Filmmaking was always a sideline, an accidental interest, even after the first film she made—in a pinch, the director who was contracted to oversee photography had his visa revoked—was lauded and for a year she was receiving invitations almost weekly to direct this or that. She said yes to one feature and then walked away, deciding she didn't like filmmaking, or didn't love it, that while the spirit and camaraderie on set were unique, the project could easily devolve into a clash of personalities. And the busywork: that was draining too. She wagered that half of one percent, at the most, of all the work she did could be judged creative, important.

Fossils were never that way. The work was all study and contemplation, even—though Sandra had never used this word to anyone but herself—rapture. That was what it was though, she thought, rapture, when you read the maps, hypothetical readouts of the past, antedating great tectonic shifts, and learned of the bygone life forms and realized how exotic our planet was, equal to anything dreamt up by the most celebrated fantasist or sci-fi writer.

She had always wanted to study marine life, but as an undergrad got phased out of the survey courses, had a professor tell her there were no jobs in it, and gradually left it behind.

It was Dale who let her do it. That was the right formulation, let, because she did need permission to pursue it, and he never flinched or expressed dismay when she told him. "When are we going to make a movie?" he had asked. "Our magnum opus."

"I think it might be never," she responded, and told him about her plan, to take postbac courses for a year or two and then apply for graduate school. And braced herself for his response, for the objections. But what he said was, of course. Of course.

Five years later she said, "Don't you think *want* is a luxury?"

But when she made this comment, she was also talking to Dale. He was having a hard time finding work. Labor Day was before the EPA commission had come in, before the music video was shot. It had been, as she recalled, five or six months since he had been hired for any jobs. Want is a luxury: she was trying to urge him not to be so particular. But he was steadfast.

"You can stop now, whenever you want," he said. "All of it. Teaching too."

"We have to have health insurance," she said.

"I suppose."

"Don't talk like this. It's bohemian live in the Village in your early twenties bullshit. And you're only doing it because I'm the one who will worry about and take care of this stuff. Things in our life that we need, that are fixed, foolproof."

"I'm just saying you have a choice," he said. "Don't ever feel like you don't have a choice. Don't you trust me?"

"Trust you to do what?"

“To take care of it. Take care of you.”

“Let me get back to you on that,” she said, and now she regretted it, being so flip. Because that was when he had done it. After seeing the printout, she was absolutely sure. That day was when he started, researching trusts, setting up her legacy.

When searching for the napkin she also found Ryan Whitehurst’s things. Initially she had put them on Dale’s desk. Now she did not know what to do with them. Throw them in the dumpster, probably. But she couldn’t bring herself to do it. Not yet.

At first she had wondered where Ryan Whitehurst found Dale’s address. But of course she would have it. From the time they met, when Dale helped shoot the car commercial in Mexico. There would be invoicing, deal memos, with all his contact information on them.

The return label said Atlas Productions, and the morning it arrived Sandra took a long time to open the package, looking at Ryan Whitehurst’s hand, the cursive, ballooning D that framed Dale’s name. She put her hand to the envelope. Something hard and square inside, like a gift card.

It was made out to Vestiture. No other name. An easy disguise, since Dale was always getting mail from production companies, there were always cables being returned, memory sticks and drives.

No doubt it was the first time they exchanged something. Or was it? Gifts Dale played by the book. He followed protocol and gave Sandra, in successive years, paper, cotton, and, a few months before he died, a piece of koa carved to resemble a turtle, with beads like braille lining the dome of its shell.

“Fifth anniversary is wood,” he announced proudly.

That turtle was now in one of the boxes in the front room.

When she tore the seal there was no gift card, rather a small framed photograph taken at sunset, at the very brink of day, the sun having slipped below the face of rimrock and a cathedral underneath with columns made of sandstone.

The caption, “What will survive of us is love.”

And there was something else inside. She tipped the envelope forward and caught it in her hand. A key ring, the metal bending slightly as she pressed her thumb over it, and the stenciled outline of a fat man in a sombrero and overalls, holding up one gloved thumb and winking.

Later in the week she got around to telling Cheryl about the money and the scholarship established in Dale's memory. "It's funny," she said, "before the funeral I thought of asking that donations be used for that. But I never liked the sound of it, the Dale Tobin scholar. I thought it would make him more anonymous, not less. I could hear the students—and I don't blame them, they're just kids, I said quite a lot of this stuff when I was their age, we all do—I could imagine them saying, Dale Tobin, who's that? And one going, beats me. Someone who died."

"Or gave the college lots of money."

"Well this is not a lot of money. Not even a quarter of the trust. But I never wanted that to happen. I never wanted him to become just someone who died."

"And what made you change your mind?"

"Other pressures. It's time to face facts. Next week there won't be a trace we ever lived here. And I decided there ought to be something."

"Oh no," Cheryl said, getting up and pouring a glass of wine. "Don't say that. People are always leaving monuments, ones they might not know about, though those are the best kind."

After Cheryl left, Sandra weighed this remark. Monuments: it was the exact sort of nonsense or pat homily she had heard far too much of over these last months, though she did not begrudge Cheryl; she knew the comment was made only to bat away the demons, to aver that life is not some postmodern comedy, not a void, though deep down, Sandra guessed, Cheryl probably knew that it was.

People say all this, she thought, it's for them, their own benefit and protection.

Then she realized what she was doing. She was quoting Ryan Whitehurst. *People say all this, they don't mean you. They mean them.* And she started to wonder if, in spite of everything, Ryan Whitehurst deserved to know. About Dale. The news did not have to come from Sandra, at least not directly. She could send a letter to Stan, Stanley, at Atlas Productions, working off the draft she used on January 4.

> Hello, and I know some of you know this already, but Dale died on New Year's. It was in a car accident and I don't have too many details and things are pretty crazy right now. Please get in touch with Reed Kovics about arrangements. I have copied him here. Thanks and love, Sandra

---

Revise it slightly, take out the date and "love Sandra" and address it to all past clients of Vestiture. The news would trickle down, sooner or later. She could send the note from her parents' house, not before. She filed it away until then.

The last box she almost labeled "Dale" before she caught herself and laughed, replacing the cap on the marker. As if she could forget. This one, stamped with the name of a moving company in Maryland, they had pilfered from a recycling dumpster in Brooklyn. None of the liquor stores and ship centers they tried had any. In it she put one of his hats, the band yellowed from sweat, plus his wallet and keys and their marriage certificate, a stain she could not identify around the seal of the state of Oregon.

When it was full, she folded the top, thinking of time capsules, the keepsakes and jewelry that were once stuffed in burial urns. Only these boxes that were going to the car were not for him. They were for her, to bring forward into the life to come.

All that was left now was the urn. The urn was the last thing she would take care of before leaving town.

On her last day she decided to take Tina to the planetarium in Portland. She did not know why—perhaps it is in the nature of last looks, Sandra thought, that we imagine we are seeing the person as they will be after we're gone—but Tina seemed to have aged considerably, running through the exhibits hall and standing in front of a virtual reality booth and spinning the ball that was in the middle of the track pad, or paying for astronaut ice cream, taking the card from Sandra and inserting it into the reader until the beep went off. They sat on the floor outside the gift shop and ate the dry, pumice-like cubes, strawberry in flavor, Sandra explaining how dairy was rehydrated but also that it was somewhat of an old conceit, and she was sure they had nice food in the space station nowadays, nicer food than what she and Tina were used to. After that they wandered around, looking at blueprints of the Mars rover, an interactive mobile that showed the distances between galaxies, where the mirrors that represented stars moved in relation to each other depending on which button you pressed. Tina paused in front of a photo of the moon. There were landmarks identified, and she put her finger on a pin that marked where one of the Apollo voyages had touched down.

"Sweetheart, I'm going to take your picture," Sandra said. "Stand there."

"Sammy, what's this?"

She could not tell if Tina was pointing to the pin or the glossy terrain around it.

"Those are seas, sweetheart."

"Seas?"

"Another word for ocean."

"You can swim on the moon?"

"No. You'd have to bring a pool. At one time though people thought that's what they were. Because from afar, without a telescope, they look like that, right?"

"What?"

"Oceans. But they're not."

"How come?"

"How come what? There's no ocean on the moon? The atmosphere, for one. The moon does not have a sky. But I'll tell you something."

"What."

"There is water there. Or was. And I suppose can be again. Buried in the poles. At the top and bottom. But right now, it's hidden. Only scientists can see it."

When it was twelve and time for the show to start, they filed into the planetarium, and Sandra found two seats in the middle. A hand guard was lowered, like a ride at an amusement park, and Sandra felt the gears rumbling beneath her as the seats tilted back and they were pointed toward the blue dome of the ceiling. After the lights went off a warning was read about cell phones and how long it takes for the eyes to become readjusted to the dark after even the briefest exposure.

"Before there was anything," said a narrator, a female voice with a British accent, "there was energy."

And then over them was the whole heavenly array, so many stars and the dandelion scud of the galaxies that for a moment Sandra forgot it was a projection. The lights pulsated and ran together, the effect like being on a ship passing by asteroids and through the dust of a supernova before entering our own solar system.

She looked at Tina, who was sucking on her fingers, her face slack with concentration.

Sandra recognized the Voyager footage of Neptune and some of the Jupiter moons and the dry pocked face of Mercury. They stopped flush against the sun, and the narrator read a history of the planets. Then they ventured out of the solar system and through a simulation of a meteor shower, the Leonids, the spidery explosions careening across the ceiling, and after what Sandra thought was a lengthy and too folksy description of light-years and parsecs—just tell them what they need, she thought, people are not so afraid of learning—an animated pencil drew a line between the stars as the voiceover identified Cassiopeia and Lyra.

Sandra and Tina traded smiles, knowing, conspiratorial, in reference to the stargazer's map Sandra had bought, and when the show ended Tina said, "That was the same one, right?"

"Cassio. Cassio?"

"Cassiopeia," Sandra finished. "She's stuck up there, right? Banished. Sent to the skies."

They lingered in front of one more exhibit, a demonstration of lift and thrust, with vacuumed blasts of air coming out of a stand of pipes, the object tilting when you attached wings to the side. Tina napped in the parking lot, and from the science museum they drove south along the river, to a house with a glassed-in patio in the back, overlooking the Eastbank Esplanade. "Look in here," Sandra said, pointing at the door. "There may be a surprise."

The surprise was Carl. He was in the back of the greenhouse, inspecting some pottery, a collection of flowerpots and saucers, for sale. He lifted Tina by the armpits and spun her around once and rested her feet on the glass case while she pointed at which flavor of custard she wanted.

Sandra had figured since they were in Portland they might as well see him, especially as he was the one who introduced Tina to the stars and planets in the first place. She had invited him to the planetarium, but he said he would not be free until early afternoon.

They greeted each other formally, with a nod, not even shaking hands, yet Sandra did not feel this formality was something she needed to fear or go out of her way to dispel.

"So you're still at your sister's then?" she asked.

"Yep," he answered. "Still there."

"I hope everything works out. Insofar as it can."

He laughed and caught himself, covering his mouth with one hand. "Sorry," he said. "I was just thinking, that's a goodbye if ever I heard one."

"Yes," Sandra said. "Yes it is."

They ordered next—Sandra chose a plate of white fudge—and went out on the pathway, past a shanty with strollers and scooters for rent, blocked by a crowd watching a team of acrobats, nine or ten in matching jeans and striped shirts, somersaulting in time to the music pumping out of a large speaker. Two wore the whiteface and lipstick of a clown and began to juggle a ball with their feet, holding it aloft through a series of flips and corkscrewed maneuvers, until another one pedaled by on a unicycle and caught it.

At the end of the performance the members of the troupe began handing out cards and DVDs and pocketing tips. Tina wandered down to the river, calling out to a family of mallards, throwing some chips of her waffle cone in the water to lure them closer.

"Sweetheart, careful," Sandra said, and tossed her plate in the trash. "You know, it's amazing. The guilt. Just that I feel for leaving."

Carl nodded, and she continued, "I can't imagine it gets easier the more you do it."

He took off his hat, inspecting the inside of it, and she could see that young as he was, baldness was already encroaching. "No," he said at last, putting it back on. "No it doesn't."

"Harder."

"Yes. Harder. Harder for her certainly."

She wondered who he meant by this. Tina. Lee. Both.

"How come you're leaving anyway, for work?"

For a moment she thought about confiding in him. She had never done it before, never talked about Dale with someone she would consider, even with the shared subject of Tina between them, a stranger. Yet she could tell he was not the sort of person to ruin the disclosure by peppering her with questions or reassurance. He would probably say nothing at all, but still, with his manner, his quiet and careful regard, find a way to acknowledge her and her loss, or do more, to honor it.

But all she said was, "Yes. Work."

Tina had stepped away from the railing. She was calling out to the ducks and edged down the slab of limestone. "Careful," Sandra repeated, but Tina didn't seem to hear her, and Sandra had to reach and caught her just as she did slip, pulling Tina back from the water with such force they both fell onto the pavement.

"Oh sweetheart," Sandra said, "Sammy's going to miss you. Big hug, okay?"

Tina put her arms around Sandra's neck, and they walked back to the ice cream shop. Carl was already in the lot, with the door of his truck open, and that was when Sandra realized she had misunderstood, that while she had counted on having Tina with her on the drive home, she would not. They would have to say goodbye here. Or no, it was worse than that. They already had.

"All is well," she texted Lee before starting the drive home. "I left them eating ice cream."

Later that afternoon the contractor arrived to complete the inspection, the same one who had visited with Beth in the first week of January. Taking him upstairs, she was afraid he would judge her work, the painting and touchups she had done. But he only nodded his head and took a few photos with the phone, then asked to be shown into the basement so he could look at the circuit box and boiler.

"Everything check out okay?" she asked back in the kitchen.

" 'As is' was a nice move," he said.

"What makes you say that?"

"I don't think that asbestos is grandfathered in. Somebody's in for a nice surprise."

When he left, she called Beth and drove to Goodwill to drop off a box. She had nothing to eat or cook in—the pots and strainer were all packed—and so she drove to the grocery as well and bought dinner at the hot bar, an orange and a salad plus a handful of bars for the road. Her last stop was the carpet cleaner's. The rug from the guest room barely fit in the car. She would have to drive with her elbow on it. Two thousand miles.

At the intersection outside her house she stopped. There was someone on her porch, dressed in a blue raincoat and jeans. Sandra put the car back into gear, and as she drove past, she saw the woman peering into the window beside the door.

She waited ten minutes in the parking lot of a gas station and when she came back the woman had not left. She was sitting in a car, a white car, with an Arizona plate.

Sandra circled the block once, and this time she pulled into the drive. She left the rug in the car, and before she was halfway up the porch walk, the woman was at the For Sale sign.

"Can you tell me who lives here?"

All she heard before opening the door and turning the deadbolt was, "Isn't this Dale Tobin's house?"

She went into the kitchen. The back was locked and so was the gate off the alley. Everything was. She had been planning on leaving within the hour.

The doorbell rang, and when it rang a second time Sandra closed her eyes. She was standing in the hall, where no one could see her. She did not know what to do. She tried to think.

She could sneak out the back door, go downtown, and then what? Even if she checked into a hotel her car was here.

She might go outside and say she was a renter, sorry, people had been coming by to ask about the house, but it was sold, under contract, and she had been instructed not to answer questions.

But this woman, Ryan Whitehurst, knew whose house it was. She had already asked about Dale Tobin. She may even know what I look like. If she's done her research. In which case no lie or feint would work.

The doorbell was still ringing, shaking the birdfeeder.

She would have to call the police, report trespassing or suspicious activity. But then Ryan Whitehurst would be detained, exonerated—there was nothing illegal about ringing a doorbell—and that would only prolong the interaction, and ensure the conversation Sandra did not want to happen would in fact take place.

The birdfeeder fell, and Sandra heard the metal clasp spinning and then stop. Ryan Whitehurst must have stepped on it. After a pause the doorbell resumed again without interruption.

Sandra opened the door.

"Whose house is this?" said Ryan Whitehurst, but Sandra did not hear these words. What she said was, "What do you want? Dale is dead."

"He is?"

"Yes. As you no doubt know. And if not, I'm sorry to break the news."

"You are the wife," said Ryan Whitehurst.

"I am the wife."

"I don't know how you could do that to somebody."

"What?"

"Even if you are the wife."

"What are you talking about?"

"I found an article that said he died on New Year's Eve. On the bridge to Washington."

"So he did. So what? You come here to tell me that?"

"I thought his friend died."

"No. It was Dale."

At this her shoulders dropped a little, and she put a hand to her brow. When she took it away, she said, "I think I am owed something. An apology. An explanation."

"Oh you do?"

"Yes."

Her hair was a lighter shade, more sunlit, than what Sandra had seen on Facebook, the blue of her eyes translucent.

"You owe me an apology," she persisted.

"Okay, you're going to have to back up," Sandra said, "and explain why you're the one who gets an explanation. When you're the one who was fucking my husband behind my back and I have to find out about it after he's gone. I mean, maybe I'm wrong, but I think you're the one who should be apologizing to me."

"There was no affair," Ryan Whitehurst said. "It never happened."

"Oh, right."

"I'm serious."

"What about the Lost Whale Inn? Isn't that this weekend? Shouldn't you be there right now?"

"Oh yeah, well what about the stuff you said? I'm moving, I'm selling the house. What about that?"

"It's true."

"It's not. It's a lie."

“Can you fucking read?” Sandra said, pointing her chin at the sign. “Can you see?”

“How many other people have you catfished?” said Ryan Whitehurst.

“How many other people what? Listen, I am obligated to let you know you are trespassing at the moment.”

“I thought you had gotten a divorce or were separated or something.”

“No. That was just your fantasy.”

“Oh my God.”

Ryan Whitehurst turned and sat on the top stair. From the jerking of her back Sandra could tell she was crying. She went and stood over her.

“Please leave,” she said. “There’s nothing for you to do here. Please go.”

“I sent a text,” she said. “To Dale.” She couldn’t go on for being short of breath, and doubled over as if she had been hit with a cramp. “There was no answer. Then I found this article. And thought, or hoped, it was a different Dale Tobin. But the details matched. His age, the movies he had done.”

“If you knew about it why did you come here?”

“Because I didn’t think it could be true.”

Ryan Whitehurst took her head out of her arms and looked at Sandra.

“Also to find out,” she said, wiping her eyes. “To find out how you could do that to somebody.”

“Funny. I was thinking the same thing.”

Sandra turned her gaze to the stop sign and watched a patrol car advance up the block. She had to remind herself she had not called the police, she had only considered doing it, and when the car parked in her drive, blocking her own vehicle, she reasoned it was a neighbor who had called them, worried the conversation with Ryan Whitehurst would somehow turn violent.

Coming out of the driver’s side was a heavyset man in a denim coat. His eyes never left Sandra, never left Ryan Whitehurst, and when the back door opened a second officer, this one in uniform, emerged. He was carrying Tina.

Sandra ran past Ryan Whitehurst. Tina reached for her, but the officer wouldn't let her go.

"What's this all about?" Sandra said.

"Are you the owner of this house?"

"I am the owner. I am Sandra Tobin."

"Would you happen to have some identification, ma'am?"

Her purse was in the car. As she opened the door she watched as the policeman in the jacket showed his badge to Ryan Whitehurst. The other began going through her mail. It had been days since she emptied the bin, and the flap wouldn't close for all the envelopes and catalogs that were inside. When she got back he was holding a folio that showed the resorts and beaches of some Mediterranean town. She handed over her license and said, "I do live here. As you can see from the mailing label."

He put Tina down. "Can you tell me who this is?" he said, pointing to Sandra.

Tina did not answer. She wore a mute and dazed expression, and he had to ask again. "Have you ever seen this woman before?"

"That's Sammy," she said at last, and put two fingers in her mouth.

"That's what she calls me," Sandra said. "I'm her babysitter. Can you tell me what's going on?"

"We are investigating reports of a kidnapping," the one in the coat said. He had stepped onto the porch.

"Kidnapping? Of this girl here?"

"When was the last time you saw her?"

"Now, today. We were in Portland today. At the planetarium. The Museum of Science and Industry."

"Would you happen to have some proof to that effect?"

Her phone was in the car too. She said, "Yes, but I'm going to take the girl inside, okay? She's cold and doesn't need to hear this. If you don't like it then we can all go inside. Ryan, I'm going to need you too."

As soon as she picked Tina up the girl wrapped her arms around Sandra's neck. She did not say anything. Sandra carried her to the couch and put her hand to her forehead.

"Do you think she's warm?"

"What?" said Ryan Whitehurst.

"Never mind. Just sit with her for a few minutes."

Sandra walked to the car again and showed them the tickets for the museum and, for good measure, in case they were doubting, the picture of Tina in front of the moon.

"So am I under arrest?" she said.

"Why would you be under arrest?" said the officer closest to her.

"For kidnapping or being an accessory to kidnapping."

"I wouldn't put it that way," he said. "When was it you saw her?"

"Two, two-thirty. I left her with her father. You can read about it here."

And she opened up the text thread to Carl. "Leaving now" was the last thing she had written, from the parking lot of the museum. "See you in a few."

"We're going to need to a copy of that," he said. "And a statement for the record."

"Now?"

"Now tends to be the best time."

"But she stays, okay? Otherwise I'm going to call my lawyer and meet you later tonight or tomorrow. It's your choice."

They looked at each other.

"Please. I don't know what more to say than please. She's pretty upset. I know. No more cops. No cruisers. Okay?"

And she went inside before they had a chance to answer. Tina still wore the same dazed expression. She said, "Sweetheart, you're at Sammy's now. Everything is okay."

There was no response. Ryan Whitehurst pushed a curl off her forehead.

"Can you say something? Sammy's getting worried."

"Sammy, where's my mommy?"

"I don't know. You tell me."

"They're looking for my mommy."

"They are?"

Tina put her fingers back in her mouth and nodded.

"I'm going to find out, okay? You wait here and I'm going to go and find out."

"Sorry to drop this on you," she said to Ryan Whitehurst. "But it won't take long. At least I hope."

Ryan Whitehurst followed her to the door. She glanced at the table, at the stack of listings Beth had left.

"Do you know what's going on?" she said.

"Not really. I have some idea, but let's hope I'm wrong."

"Sammy, don't go!" Tina shouted, as if she had not understood what was happening before. She ran to Sandra and clutched her legs. She wouldn't let go.

"I won't be long, sweetheart. And you stay here with Ryan. Can I tell you something? Let go of Sammy's legs, and I'll tell you something."

"What?"

She bent down and whispered, "She knew him. Dale. She saw him."

"It's true," said Ryan Whitehurst.

"And she's going to tell you all about him. You wait here and listen. If you don't let me go then I can't go and find out about mommy."

"Just do your best" she said, getting up. "And if push comes to shove you can always put a screen in front of her."

"Roger that," said Ryan Whitehurst.

The officers had not left the porch. She asked if she could take her own car, and they said yes, Thirtieth Street station. She waited for them to leave and before backing out of the driveway tried Carl. The call went straight to voice mail and she typed, "Not sure where you are, but Tina is safe."

Then, while she was on her way to the station, she dialed Richard Rawlings. "Whatever happens," she said, giving an account that even then she recognized as garbled to the point of being incomprehensible, since she was still not sure what had happened, "I don't want her to leave the house. They can't hold her, can they, not indefinitely?"

"Not indefinitely," he said. "But it's certainly at their pleasure. They can bring her in as long as the investigation lasts."

He named an attorney who specialized in criminal cases. Dan Blue.

"That's easy to remember, right?"

"Yes," she said. "It is easy. Can you call him?"

"Are you at the police station now?"

"No. Going."

"What do you want me to tell him?"

"I don't know. Just be ready, I guess. In case."

"In case of what?"

"That's what I'm about to find out."

At the precinct there was no sign of the officers who questioned her at the house. She sat on a felt chair in a brightly lit bay, scanning missing signs that were taped to the wall, some stretching as far back as 1986. The hairstyles dated. A few of the locations where the person was last reported seen franchises that no longer existed.

After thirty minutes she got up and wandered into the break room, somewhat surprised that no one stopped her. The tables were empty. A Formica countertop with a box of plastic spoons and a looped holder of sugar packets. The coffee machine was automatic, and she pressed the button for milk and sugar and watched the spray dart against the lid of the plastic cup.

Settling into the same chair, she saw she had a text.

"Things are okay," it said. "Squad car out front."

She did not recognize the number. She thought perhaps it was Richard Rawlings's cell phone and was ready to check it in her call history before realizing it was Ryan Whitehurst. Still not certain, she typed, "Spotify Elmo playlist always a good one."

"Kk."

"She doesn't know the police are out there does she?"

"No," wrote Ryan Whitehurst.

Sandra's phone number was not in any of the emails. She must have found it in one of the boxes, on an old bill or insurance card.

No. The kitchen. When she and Dale had gone to Banff and rented out the house for two weeks they wrote their numbers down on a legal pad and taped the page inside the cabinet closest to the sink. For emergencies.

She was summoned to a desk on the other side of the foyer, and a man who introduced himself as Sergeant Mallison. His oxford was bluing from sweat, and he made notes with a heavy sterling pen. On the desk in front of him was a calendar with leather corners, the names of holidays in the squares, one week whose days had been X'ed out in red ink. She also saw, closer, under his arm, a photograph of Carl's truck. She recognized the clamp-on mirrors and the paint gone from the lettering on the gate. The picture was black and white and grainy, and she was sure it had been taken at a traffic stop. The time stamp read five-twenty.

She saw that he had been watching her. He said, "Does that look familiar?"

"Sure. It's his."

"His?"

"Carl Featherstone. I'm not sure if it belongs to him, but that's the truck he drives."

"Why don't you tell me what's going on?" he said. "I think we would all appreciate that."

"I don't think I can. Where is the girl's father?"

"The father is in custody."

Exactly how Lee drew it up, she thought. For it had to have been her. Sandra could see no other hand in this, and why else would those officers let Tina stay at her house?

"We had half the state of Oregon looking for that girl."

"Where was she found?"

"At a McDonald's. We had a nice little scene there, at that McDonald's."

"I bet."

"He says you were with her."

"I was," Sandra said. "For much of the morning, then I dropped her off."

"May I see your phone?"

Ryan Whitehurst had sent another update, but Sandra did not check it. She typed in her code and handed him the phone and he began reading her texts, thumbing down, making notes with the silver pen.

She thought back to what she had written to Carl. Let's have lunch after, before we go back, leaving now, see you in a few. Nothing incriminating, unless he was inclined to deduce Carl had freelanced and illegally taken custody of the girl.

Which may not be wholly untrue, she reflected. Though as far as she knew Lee and Carl were still not divorced and there was no official agreement to observe. Were mediation pacts binding?

Mallison did not seem to be in any kind of hurry. He was still scrolling down with his thumb. "Listen," Sandra said, "can I be straight with you?"

"I don't know," he said. "Can you?"

"What are you trying to find? Clearly there was no kidnapping."

"No," he said, and turned back to the phone. "I guess there wasn't."

Now another officer came over and sat on the edge of the desk. He pretended to touch the brim of his cap at her and swung one of his legs, knocking it against the seat of Sandra's chair.

"Detective Sharp," said the sergeant.

Sharp asked her to recite what happened, and she wondered if it was a test, if they were keeping tabs of the faithfulness of her account, comparing one version to the next. Maybe it was not a test, maybe it was simply policy, a way to find clues. Charting the variances, details that suddenly appear or are elided.

"You said you picked her up at nine," he said. "Where?"

"She came to my house. Her mom brought her."

Sharp was older, she noticed, yet he would defer to the sergeant, pausing before each question, as if to be sure it was his turn to speak.

"When was the last time you saw her?" he said.

"Lee? I just told you."

The sergeant raised his head.

"Ever notice anything about her that was unusual?" he said. "Signs of wayward behavior, depression, anxiety."

"Do you really think that's all that unusual, sergeant?" Sandra asked.

He smiled, an expression of apology or impatience or both.

"Anything that might help, that's all."

"She made the call, right?"

It was only a guess, but she knew it to be true, knew it with the fiercest intuition.

Sharp waited for the sergeant to answer. And he did: "Why would that matter?"

"I was thinking you could trace the signal or something."

"In order to . . ."

"Track her down," Sandra said.

"Yes. Yes, thank you. We will look into that. So is this the last communiqué," he said, reading the date and time of her most recent text with Lee. "You have not heard from her since she dropped the girl off?"

"For the third time no," said Sandra.

"Now what about this?"

Sharp handed her the printout of a text. "I took her home, but Lee's still not here." Sandra read it a few times before recognizing it as one of her own, sent on the night she brought Tina to the trailer and Lee wasn't at home.

"Can you tell us what happened?"

"Then? I don't remember," Sandra said. "It was a while ago. Probably some mishap in communication, no big deal. About the drop-offs."

"Okay then." He handed the phone to Sharp and said he would call her later tonight or first thing in the morning. He gave her a card and said that was the line to this desk and wrote down another number in pencil. This one he would pick up anytime, he explained. If she ever saw Lee Haynesworth again, she was to call him right away.

She wondered, she hoped, he was using such language only to underscore the severity of the situation, trying to be sure she wouldn't go home and throw the card in the trash or forget all about it. She assured him if she saw Lee again she would call. He nodded.

She followed the detective down a hall to a room with a bank of monitors. Some were security cams, others showed virtual reality or time lapse sequences. Lighted amoebic shapes bent and swam. He sat before a screen at the end and opened Decipher TextMessage, the watermark of the police shield disappearing, and highlighted the thread from Carl and the one from Lee and uploaded her messages into the police database. When he took the cable out of the phone he said she was free to go.

On the street she read the text from Ryan Whitehurst.

"Nothing in the fridge?" it said.

Before typing back she called Richard Rawlings again.

"That was fast," he said.

"Didn't feel like it. Let me ask you something. What's the penalty for calling 911 for no reason?"

"Is that what happened here?"

"I think so. Is it something I should worry about?"

"No. Generally it's a misdemeanor."

"But what if?"

"What if what?"

"There are priors. Other incidents involved. I don't know. I'll keep you posted."

She thanked him and turned back to the thread from Ryan Whitehurst. "Order anything you want," she wrote. "I'll pay for it obviously."

"K, and just so you know, asleep now," came the response.

"Asleep? For real?"

It had been almost an hour since Sandra received the last text.

"Do you want to leave?" she typed, but before she sent it figured she may as well call Cheryl and make sure she was available to go and watch Tina.

"Hey there," Cheryl said when Sandra called, "you across the line yet?" From the shouting and sound of glasses and silverware Sandra knew she was at Lighting Works.

"No, I haven't left yet."

"I was just thinking about you. Some chap here said he worked with Dale on a project. Years ago. A documentary with Mel."

"Some chap where?"

"You know we got that event tonight. It's the Thunderbirds auction."

"What time does it get over?" Sandra asked.

A thump on the line. Sandra had to pull the phone away from her ear.

"At this point let's just hope it does end," Cheryl said. "If you're still here you should come down."

Sandra said yeah, maybe she would, and when she hung up deleted what she had written to Ryan Whitehurst. Now all she wrote was, "Still asleep?"

"Out cold."

"I'm done with the cops," Sandra wrote. "I'll try and be home as soon as I can."

She drove to Butte Farms, though she knew Lee would not be there. But she had the key and thought perhaps in the trailer there would be some clue to her whereabouts. A patrol car was parked a block away. Sandra did not even slow but turned at the end of the street and took a right out of the trailer park. She could not think of where to go except the bars downtown. After making a circle around Eighth Street and skirting the waterfront it occurred to her that Lee might have the sense to ditch the car after making the emergency call.

Porter's, the coffee shop where Sandra had met Tina, was closing. A waitress was putting chairs on top of the tables, and another was lifting bills from a tray and tapping on a hand calculator.

There was the friend Lee had mentioned, LuAnn, but Sandra possessed no other information about her, not a last name or address. All she knew was what Lee had said, that she worked at the Mini Mart. She drove to the one on Marine Drive and the clerk who was on said he had no idea who Sandra was talking about. She received the same response when checking the laundromat next door, and when she called the Mini Mart in Warrenton she kept hearing a busy signal and realized it would be quicker just to drive over.

She stood in line behind a woman buying lottery tickets. She had already purchased two and was considering a third, and finally Sandra stepped to the cashier and said, "Listen, I'm sorry, I'm looking for someone. It's kind of an emergency. Does anyone named LuAnn work here?"

"LuAnn Bae," said the woman, and Sandra replied sure, that was the one.

Her shift started at eleven thirty. An hour from now.

She drove to the marina at Skipanon. The gate to the parking lot was open, and she heard an outboard lapping the water as a boat docked in the slip ahead of her. A dog hopped off the bow.

"How's our girl," she texted to Ryan Whitehurst.

"She's up now."

"Do you want me to come home?"

"Do what you have to do."

"Has she said anything about tonight?"

"She keeps asking about her mommy."

"Her sleeping you don't think is a sign of shock or something?"

"I'm not a doctor," said Ryan Whitehurst.

Sandra looked at the clock on the dash: 10:48. Four minutes later her phone buzzed again.

"Is that what yr worried about, shock?"

"I don't know," she wrote. "Kinda."

It was how Tina looked when the officers brought her to the porch, the frozen mask of bewilderment. Had she tensed or lashed out or broken down, Sandra might somehow feel better. The undisturbed face, the hesitation before she spoke, that was what gave Sandra pause.

"I can be home whenever," she wrote.

"Is she allergic to anything?"

"No," Sandra said.

"So what is going on with the mom?"

"Still looking," said Sandra. "Just tell her Sammy's working on it."

She could not wait any longer. At the store she found LuAnn eating pizza in one of the booths, was able to identify her by the red coveralls she had already put on for her shift. She was older than Sandra expected, with a gray ponytail and rings on four of her fingers, one large enough to contain the replica of what looked like an oil portrait or votive mural.

"I know you don't know me from a hole in the ground," she said, "but Lee is missing right now. Nobody can find her."

LuAnn drew a cross over her chest.

"Do you know where she could be?"

"I have not seen her. Last time, last time she was just driving around."

"Driving around?"

"He put her on a suicide watch."

"I don't know anything about this," Sandra said. "For how long?"

"I don't know. Carl had to stay the week." She tapped her rings against the table. "That was sort of the point," she said. "You get my meaning?"

"Can you call her? I've tried. Maybe she's screening my number."

LuAnn took her phone out of the front pocket of her coveralls and held it to her ear before putting it back on the table. She shook her head.

"Where does she like to go?" Sandra said. "Bars. Friends' places. Anywhere she could be right now."

"Lee likes to drink at home. She don't really drink downtown. You can try Workman's. And that place next to the brewery. In the old bank or whatever."

There was nothing else around, so Sandra wrote her number down on a coupon for an auto supply store. It was after eleven, and she did not want to check bars one by one but that is what she did. She tried the two LuAnn named. The first was having an open mic, and Sandra thought she saw Lee, and even approached the woman only to see that up close she looked nothing like Lee, it had only been something in her profile, or a shared mannerism maybe, like the way she slid a coaster down the bar at one of her friends, flicking it the way a dealer would at a casino.

She tried four more places before going to the trailer again. The squad car was gone. She knocked on the door, and when there was no answer, she let herself in. She pulled on the wire and the bulb singed out. By the light of her phone she saw a bottle of vodka open on the table. She tried calling Lee again. There was no answer. On the refrigerator she pinned a note that said, "Lee, call me soon, Sandra" and poured what little was left of the vodka down the sink and rinsed the bottle and put it in the trash. She sat on the couch and tried to think.

What if she wasn't in Astoria at all. She may have bolted, called the cops, and taken a bus for who knows where. She would have to go home, and when Tina woke spin some invention, tell her she was going back to Portland to stay with her dad.

Except her dad, quite possibly, was under arrest.

She may also be dead. Sandra was surprised at how quickly that option came to her. It must be because she was out of choices, out of ideas. There was nothing to do now but call the police and see if they had been able to find her. Her or her body.

She took out the card the sergeant had given her and had entered the first three digits of his number when she remembered Chu, Lee's neighbor. It was the last place she could check. She drove around the block before realizing she would have no way of recognizing the trailer from the front and went back and parked in the same spot and walked across Lee's yard, past the sandbox and swing set.

The back door was open. She rasped on the screen.

No one came, though she heard voices, or she thought she did. She turned around, looking at the toys in the sandbox, and when the light came on behind her she saw something in the flowerbed. What resembled a clamp for a tube or drainage pipe, except the ends were tasseled. Walking closer Sandra saw it was a shoe.

"Lee," she said, bending down, listening to the hum and wheeze of her breathing. "Lee."

She tried again, tapping her shoulder. Chu was behind her now, wearing a shower cap and a sweatshirt. "You go back to bed," she said through the screen.

"Sorry," Sandra said. "I didn't mean to disturb you."

The woman did not answer. She craned her head to one side to try and get a look at Lee's face.

"You see her today?" Sandra asked.

"She said she was coming over."

"She almost made it."

Chu helped get her to the car, waiting while Sandra ran back to the street and drove almost onto her lawn. At first Sandra tried to carry Lee, but her back foot gave out and they went to the ground together. They rested her arms on their shoulders then, Lee's legs dragging beneath them. She woke for a second, said "Hey," and slapped Sandra's face. By the time they got her in the passenger seat she was out again.

In the dome light Sandra saw that Lee's eyebrow was scratched, and a trace of blood had run down one cheek and dried. Sandra tried to scrub it away with a fingernail. What she could. Then she pulled the hoodie down. Lee's shirt was untucked. You could see the skin around her waist.

She parked not on her own street but the one next to it since that was a shorter path to the house. She used the back door. The stove light was on and Tina was asleep. So was Ryan Whitehurst, in the easy chair. Her computer was at her feet, and when Sandra went to close it she saw the laptop was connected to a drive—one of Dale's drives, which she had planned to save, labeled 2/2018.

She nudged Ryan Whitehurst, who pinched the bridge of her nose and took a slow, weary scan of the room.

"You find her?" she whispered.

"Outside," said Sandra. "I need your help."

Lee remained still when they lifted her from the car, Sandra with her arms around her chest and Ryan Whitehurst there to catch her feet. They brought her in that way, like two robbers in a vaudeville act, and though the storm door clapped shut behind them Tina did not stir. In the guest room Sandra unzipped Lee's hoodie. Ryan Whitehurst took it and held it halfway to her nose and asked where the laundry was.

"Behind you," Sandra said.

They left her jeans on. Each of them unlaced a shoe and Sandra pulled a blanket up to Lee's chin and turned off the light.

"You wait here," Ryan Whitehurst whispered in the hall. "I'll go to the grocery."

Sandra went and sat in the easy chair. It was still warm from when Ryan Whitehurst had slept in it, and after a few moments she got up to inspect the kitchen. Ryan Whitehurst had ordered delivery from one of the Italian kitchens in town and Sandra ate some of the leftover penne. Then she went to check on Lee one more time and crossed the hall to her own room.

In the night Tina started to howl. Sandra did not know if she was catching the first scream or the second, for she could already hear Ryan Whitehurst asking what was wrong. The fit only redoubled when she came into the living room and Tina saw her.

"What is it, sweetheart?" she asked, picking Tina up.

"I think it was a dream," said Ryan Whitehurst. "A bad dream, right Tina?"

Tina nodded, clenching her face, trying to stop the tears.

"Did it have a monster in it?" Sandra asked.

Tina shook her head. She was taking short, labored inhalations, staring at Sandra as the tears fell.

"Bad guys?"

"They're all gone now," said Ryan Whitehurst, rubbing her back. "It's okay. You're safe. No bad guys here."

"I want my mommy."

"Well that's good," Sandra answered. "Because your mommy's right here."

"She is?"

"I'll show you. But she's sleeping, okay? We have to be very quiet."

Tina bunched up her face and nodded. Sandra and Ryan Whitehurst took her hands and they tiptoed down the hallway. Sandra pushed the door of the guest room until the light fell on Lee's ankles.

"I want to sleep with her," Tina said.

"Oh no, Sammy's going to sleep with you, okay? Sammy's going to sleep with you, and Ryan's going to watch for the bad guys."

She asked Tina if she could turn the couch back into the fort, and Tina showed Sandra and Ryan Whitehurst how to do that, giving instructions on where the cushions should go and where the vulnerable points of the fortification might be.

"Don't let them get my daddy," Tina said.

"What about your daddy?" asked Sandra, and Ryan Whitehurst mouthed the word "police" and held out her arms, as if it was a question.

"We won't," said Sandra. "Ryan's going to stay up all night, aren't you Ryan?"

"All night."

She hugged Tina then and waited for Ryan Whitehurst to turn off the lights. It was the first time Sandra had lay down beside someone since Dale died, and she was the one to fall asleep first, for when the weight of Tina fell on her she woke, not knowing what had happened. She could not see her in the dark, and when she woke for a second time Tina was on her chest and the curtains rimmed with light. She had no feeling in one arm and tilted her shoulder until Tina slid off to one side.

Ryan Whitehurst was at the stove, stirring something, eggs and some kind of potato hash or casserole. She must have bought the pan, Sandra realized, seeing that plastic plates were also on the table.

"Hey there," said Ryan Whitehurst. Sandra noticed she had changed shirts. This one she recognized, from the tear in the collar, as one of her own.

"Sorry," said Ryan Whitehurst, looking down. "I got some puke on me last night."

"That's no problem."

She must have found it in her room. Which meant if she had gone back to sleep, she had done it in Sandra's bed.

Ryan Whitehurst turned back to the stove and Sandra reached around her for the mug that was on the drying rack and found a spoon and took some instant coffee out of the box that was open on the counter. She lifted the kettle off one of the boilers and poured the water in.

"I'll be outside," she said, taking her fleece off the nail.

"Okay. Breakfast is almost ready."

On the stair Sandra sat huddled in her fleece, looking at the rings the porcelain made on the concrete. The sun was hidden, but gulls were circling overhead and she could tell the marine layer would burn off. In one hour. It was one of those mornings.

On this try Carl answered.

"You sleep in the big house?" she asked.

"Thought I was going to for a while there. They let me go."

"Good. Tina is here."

There was a pause, then he said, "I guess there wasn't no other option."

"She's safe. I'm not sure about anything else, but she's safe. Lee's here too."

"Lee's there? At your house?"

"That's right."

"Well I think I'll let the police know that."

"No. No you won't."

"They want to know. I'm supposed to check in with them at eight o'clock."

"And when you do say everything's all right. A big misunderstanding, just a clusterfuck if we're being honest, but it's straight now and you're on your way down here."

"Why would I do that, when I been waiting for this? This is the end."

"Maybe. Maybe it is the end. But not the way you figure. What time can you get down here?"

"I was just about to leave when you called."

"What time can you get down here? I'll get Lee up and in the best shape I can."

"I'm not going to see her."

"Yes. You have to."

"She called the cops on me, you get that? We were driving around and she saw the playground at McDonald's and asked if we could stop and I was standing there ordering—"

"Look, I get it," Sandra said. "I'm not saying it's not terrible. Or that if I were you I wouldn't want to press charges. I mean, it's not a big deal, calling 911, it's just a fine, but you could get a pretty favorable custody agreement, I understand that. But that's not what you're going to do. Lee needs some help, and she's going to get it. In the meantime, a cease-fire. And the two of you are going to talk to Tina. You can't keep her in the dark anymore."

"And say what?"

"I don't know. Level with her. Try to unwind yesterday's nightmare."

"Just going to end up with a new nightmare. Tina could hear her yesterday."

"Hear her what?"

"Rambling. Yelling. She called me shit faced. You don't think she'd call 911 without running it by me first?"

"What a dumpster fire. Well let's just hope yesterday's a blur and Tina can shake it off. You tell her Mommy's going away, call it a vacation if you like, just plant the seed, and meanwhile you guys are going to live at your sister's place. Are they coming back any-time soon?"

"June at the earliest."

"Right, so you drive over here, and I'll get Lee ready, okay?"

When there was no reply she said, "If you don't, I'm going to back up Lee's story. I'm going to say you weren't supposed to take her and when I dropped her off it was a total shock and yeah, it's melodramatic to call the cops but Lee got scared and considering the circumstances I don't think it's all that weird for a mom to do."

"They won't believe you."

"They might. You want to find out? Let's go."

"Tell me why you're doing this," he said. "For Tina, that's what you're going to say."

"That's part of it."

"What's the other?"

"Some messes can't be fixed," Sandra said. "Some can. At least partway. And I'm not ready to give up on this one."

There were more calls to make, but it was early. In the kitchen Ryan Whitehurst was sipping coffee. There was some creamer on the table, and Sandra reached and poured some of it into her mug. As she did she saw Ryan Whitehurst was holding the key ring she had sent to Dale. Sent to her.

"Do you know what this is?" she asked.

Sandra went to the door and listened for the sound of Tina's breathing. Once she heard it, she came back and sat at the table beside Ryan Whitehurst.

"A good luck charm I suppose," Sandra said. "One with personal significance for the two of you."

"Dale won it. At Skee-Ball."

"Skee-Ball. Like at an arcade?"

"There was an arcade there, yes," Ryan Whitehurst said, turning it over to the side with the logo on it. "It really is tremendously racist," she said. "Don't you think?"

"I guess," Sandra said.

"Dale said it must have been old and they couldn't get rid of their back stock."

"Where was it?"

"In Mexico. On the border, not far from Nogales. One of those cantinas that are like a tourist trap, with more Americans in it than anyone else. We didn't hear a word of Spanish. The place was filled with this bachelor party contingent, and we played pool against them, me and Dale. He never said anything about this?"

"No."

"We were stuck there, though we didn't know it. By the time we did it was one o'clock in the morning."

"When you were shooting," Sandra asked. "The commercial?"

"Yes. And on our way home the van broke down. Javier pulled off on one of those turnaround connectors the cops use, though in Mexico I'm not sure what they are for, and he was turning the van on and off like something was broke. And the gauges were broke. Pretty much everything was. The dash said the van was overheating, though it wasn't that hot out, and Javier had checked the coolant. It's the alternator, he said, and Stan, who was a couple miles ahead, came back and when we got out there was an enormous pool beneath the van like it was leaking something. Dale volunteered to stay behind, and I was like no, that's not right, he's pickup crew, so I said I would stay too. To be honest Javier should have stayed, he was the one who knew the most about cars or trucks, but he did not, and we moved the equipment to the other van and they drove off and it was almost nine when the wrecker arrived and the guy took one look at it and said kaput. Not the alternator but a problem with one of the belts. And we rode with him back to the shop, and he said he couldn't guarantee that he would have it ready in time for morning or the next day at all and it was too late to rent something to drive back that night. Stan at this point was through customs, and when we called he was pretty cool, he was like, go to the casino, the company will spot you a couple hundred in chips and there was like a Fairfield Inn across the street, and he told us he would make a reservation and then find a van for us to drive in the morning.

"So we went into the cantina to wait for the shuttle. The casino shuttle or the hotel shuttle. Dale had called them, and they said it would be an hour or close to it. I ordered a beer and Dale I think had tequila, a liberal pour, I remember that, and there was this mariachi band playing 'Take On Me' and 'Walking in Memphis' and all these other '80s songs. I think the bachelor party had brought them. So we started playing games, we got into that pool match, but we were both terrible; in one whole game we could only knock in a ball or two. Then we tried one of those games where the joystick moves a claw and you try to pick a ball or a stuffed animal out of the pile, and that was when Dale saw the Skee-Ball machines, and he said, watch, I'm heavyweight champion of this, and I said, big talker, but it was true, he kept getting the ball in the center ring or the one just below it, and each time he did the machine spat out tickets, light blue tickets, like at the Putt-Putt when I was a kid, and he had a humongous roll of them and we took them up to the counter and were like, what can I get with this. Dale tried to order a drink with the tickets. Por favor, he said. Tequila por favor. But of course you couldn't use them for that, and in spite of what he had won, anything at the counter worth getting was like one thousand points, and he had four hundred, and for that there was really no option except this key chain. So he got that and we started laughing about the man on one side. It was the logo for the place, and we decided his name was Paco. So for the rest of the night it became a joke, Where's Paco, where's Paco?"

The first email she had read.

> Wish I had photos to share—Carol said we should take some to prove we left the beach for more than five minutes but we didn't. So there you go.
>
> And no sign of Paco. I looked.

"And now it was clear no one was coming to get us, so we walked to the hotel across the street. We thought we were lucky they had a vacancy, but then we realized that was because it was such a dump. We had to wait five minutes for the clerk, and we only got one room because it was the company's dollar, and Dale was making all these jokes about *The Shining*, and it sort of freaked me out too. When we got in and saw there was only one bed, we were both like, fuck it, we'll be up in four hours anyway."

"You slept in the same bed?"

"Yeah, but nothing happened. No fooling around. I'm sort of amazed now, considering we were both hammered. But I suppose I knew he was married. Sorry, I know you don't want to hear any of this right now."

"Then what happened?"

"Nothing. I woke him up. Or tried to, I tried to wake him up to watch the sunrise. At like six. Living in LA, you're in the desert all the time, but you never see anything like this. The sun hitting the slope of the mountains, the parking lot was like it was covered in snow or frost. And he sat up and opened his eyes and then dove back down and went to sleep. All in one move."

"Yes," said Sandra. "I have seen that move many times. Then what?"

"About an hour later we rented the new van. The line at customs was nil, and he was able to make his flight. I remember that. He was flying out of Tucson at noon.

"Here," she said.

"No," Sandra answered. "I don't want it. You keep it."

Ryan Whitehurst put the key ring in the pocket of her jeans and said, "There was no affair. You have to believe me."

"But you wanted one. You wanted to go to the Lost Whale Inn."

"Not when he was alive. Then it was different. I mean, it's not like we didn't talk about it, or start to. I said I didn't want to feel like an applicant to a filled position. Meaning you."

Sandra remembered that line as well from one of the emails. Ryan Whitehurst had written, "That's one post I don't care if it's filled or not."

"And what did he say?"

"He said the problem was I wasn't married."

"What does that mean?"

"I'm not sure. I've tried to figure it out and now I know that I never will. Maybe that people who aren't married don't understand marriage. They romanticize it, I mean I know I do, but if I was married I would know better, and there wouldn't be any kind of, language barrier I guess you would call it, between us.

"But this is just a guess. We never talked about it again. And he never, well you know he never made a move."

"I always thought something happened in Seattle."

"In Seattle? I never saw Dale in Seattle."

"At that conference hosted by Boeing. I read the notes. They said, I'll be at the plenary, I'll try to find you after."

"It never worked out. We were scattered, the team I mean, trying to get this movie off the ground."

Tina walked into the kitchen, in the same clothes, the long sleeve shirt with the stars on the shoulder, that she had worn to the planetarium, her hair shooting off in all directions.

"Where's my mommy?" she asked.

"I'm going to check," Sandra said. "You stay and play with Ryan, okay?"

Lee was still sleeping in the guest bed. Sandra knew she would need more than one outfit. Tina too, for that matter.

No one was on the road, and she was at Butte Farms inside of ten minutes. In the trailer she could not find a suitcase or duffel, so she used old shopping bags. For Lee she packed another pair of jeans, khakis, and two shirts, the lavender one with the sleeves cut off and a collared blouse that would do in case she needed it for formal occasions, though Sandra could not think of what those might be.

She also packed Tina's shirts and a dress with a felt dinosaur on it and her Etch A Sketch and block toys. Before leaving she sat once more on the couch and dialed Best Day. It was not yet nine and no one answered, but the recording gave a number to call in case it was an emergency, and when she dialed that she was grateful it reached someone other than Jenny Travers. Perhaps Deirdre, the partner Jenny had mentioned. Sandra said she was looking for a recommendation, "a place in Portland ideally, where this person—my friend—can dry out and maybe talk about other stuff too. But it has to be right away. It has to be today."

"Okay, let me see what I can scrounge up," the voice said. "What did you say your name was?"

"Sandra Tobin. Lee Haynesworth is the person I mentioned. I'll call you back in like an hour?"

"We'll call you. And these places, they tend to be high-toned."

"What does that mean, expensive?"

"Yes. Expensive."

"Payment," Sandra said, thinking of Dale and his check, "payment will not be a problem."

When she got home Ryan Whitehurst and Tina were in the backyard. She opened the curtains over the sink and saw they were blowing bubbles on the back stoop. Tina jumped to pop the highest one with the wand.

Sandra went into the guest room and sat at the foot of the bed. The hair around Lee's ears was matted with sweat, and she could smell the vomit and booze lifting off her clothes. She went into the bathroom to get the shower going.

"Lee," she said, shaking her by the shoulders. "Lee, it's Sandra."

Lee turned over and lolled her tongue around her mouth.

"Do you know where you are? I picked you up," Sandra said. "I brought you here last night."

"Is that Teenie? I can hear Teenie."

She saw the marks on her forehead again, as she had when she first saw Lee at Best Day and taken them to be signs of windburn.

"That's her. Come on Lee. We got to take a shower."

"I want to see her. Is she outside?"

"Let's get cleaned up first," Sandra said. "You don't want her to see you like this."

She put out her hand, and Lee took it and walked into the bathroom, a slight hitch or limp to her gait. With her palm she wiped the steam from the mirror, and Sandra could tell she didn't like what she saw. She dabbed the edge of her lips with her thumb.

"You might want to leave," she said.

"Are you going to throw up?"

"No."

"Then it's nothing I haven't seen before," said Sandra, and Lee took off her shirt and put her hand in the spray to test the water and stepped into the shower and closed the curtain.

Sandra put the lid of the toilet down and sat.

"Am I in trouble?" Lee asked.

"I don't think so. Not with the law. But you got to get help, Lee. You can't be doing this, calling 911."

"What did you tell Teenie?" Lee asked.

"Not a thing," said Sandra. "It's not for me to tell."

She could see Lee was not doing anything except standing under the water.

"Can you wash, Lee? Carl's on his way. He'll be here any minute."

"Oh God."

"And you're going to drive back together. To Portland. And check into a place."

Through the curtain she saw Lee's arms stop moving and her head drop.

"It's that or never see Tina again, or see her *x* many times a year, with who knows what kind of supervision, a cop or chaperone accompanying you. Is that what you want? I'm sure you understand this won't turn out in your favor. Not now. Not with this police department file."

"I don't think Carl will agree to that."

"He already has."

Ryan Whitehurst knocked on the door. She was carrying Sandra's coffee. "Stay," Sandra said to her and walked to the front of the house and pulled a towel out of one of the boxes and handed it to Lee. She showed her the grocery bags, and Lee chose an outfit, the lavender tee and some chinos she had to stretch in order to get the button in front but still made a whole lot of difference, Sandra thought.

"Okay, we're just about halfway home," said Sandra. "Can you get the moisturizer that's on the sink?"

When Ryan Whitehurst brought it, Sandra said, "I don't have any makeup. I packed mine."

"I have some," said Ryan Whitehurst and went out.

Sandra pumped the lotion onto her hands.

"I was just trying to get him to see me," Lee said, holding her wrists. "I know that's crazy but it's what I was thinking."

"It's not crazy," said Sandra. "Believe me, I know. Now look up."

She began smoothing the lotion onto Lee's face, and Ryan Whitehurst returned with a leatherette case. "I'm almost out of concealer," she said, "but there should be enough," and she daubed the cream on the splotches beneath Lee's eyes while Sandra wetted the towel and scrubbed off what was left of the blood. She picked through Ryan Whitehurst's travel kit. There was a pencil in here too, and she was about to put it to Lee's eyes when the phone rang. It was Jenny Travers.

"Can you finish up?" she said to Ryan Whitehurst. In the kitchen Tina hardly noticed her. Ryan Whitehurst had set her phone against the mug and cued up an episode of *Sesame Street*.

"So you heard?" she said.

"I heard you called," said Jenny, "and I was able to find a place. This clinic, it's in the Pearl District. I sent them the file we had on Lee."

"Thank you," Sandra answered. "Can you tell them she'll be there this afternoon?"

Next she took out the card from the police station and called the number written in pencil. Mallison answered on the third ring.

"So, I've been thinking," she said, "and this whole thing is my fault. You know, I should have texted that he was taking her for the day, that there was a change in plans. I blew it. I fucked up."

"You don't have to say that," he said. "Meantime, we are still searching."

"No, I found her," Sandra said. "She's here. The husband too. All of them."

"All three of them? What's his status?"

"He was hot but not so much anymore. I talked to him. Do you want his number?"

"I got it," Mallison said and hung up.

Sandra heard Carl's truck, heard it idle before the engine shut off. She put her hand in Tina's hair and went out to the porch. He had his back to her, and she could see his breath fogging in the cold.

"Okay," she said. "They're both in there."

"What about the police? Tina?"

"Too early to tell. She's exhausted. Comatose really. But rallying. Here."

She gave him the slip of paper with the address of the facility on it.

"I gave Lee conditions," she said. "I said you wouldn't press charges or sue for a vindictive custody agreement, but she had to get help. You do that, she does this. Okay? And I'm not asking you to do anything else. Just go in there and be civil. But not until I come and get you."

Ryan Whitehurst had managed to get Lee into the kitchen. The effect of the brightener was startling, and Sandra guessed that Ryan must have been asked to apply makeup on set from time to time. Tina was holding one of Lee's hands. The other was shaking. Sandra set her mug down and wrapped Lee's fingers around it.

"Give me any of that," said Lee, eyeing the skillet Ryan Whitehurst had brought over, "it'll just come back up."

"I'll set it down here," said Ryan Whitehurst, putting an oven mitt down first.

"Mommy, do you want some tomatoes?" Tina asked.

"Yeah," Lee said. "Yeah I think I can manage those."

"How about another juice box?" Ryan Whitehurst said to Tina.

"I'll take one of them," Lee said.

She was keeping her eyes trained on the door. As if Carl would walk through at any moment.

"Well I guess I'll go and get him," Sandra said. "I just wanted to be sure you were ready."

When she went outside Carl was sitting on the stairs. She did not follow him into the kitchen but waited until he said, "Hi, Lee," and she heard Tina shout, "We're having breakfast!" Then she stepped outside. Ryan Whitehurst came out the front door. "Let's not crowd them," Sandra said, and since there was nowhere to go, they ended up sitting in the rental car. Sandra thought she might find some preparations for the Lost Whale Inn, but all there was to see was a copy of the rental agreement folded in the cup holder.

"So when did you find out about the emails?" she said. "That I was the one sending them."

"Not until I got here, I guess. I had some doubts but managed to talk myself out of them. I thought it was weird when I sent the gift, the key chain, and he didn't seem to know what it was, or you didn't seem to know what it was. But then I was like, I just remember that night better, it's not to him what it is to me, and anyway he was hammered. Then the Fillmore shoot fell through, and I texted Dale to say I would be there early and he never answered, so I emailed and got an error message. That's when I started getting suspicious. Worried in fact. So I did a Google news search and the story about the accident came up, but it was behind a paywall, and then I found the funeral notice."

"The funeral notice? I didn't know there was one."

"Yeah. Dale Tobin. What was his middle name, Frank or something?"

"Francis."

"It had his name on it and the dates and address of the church."

"His mother must have done that," Sandra said. "Or the church."

"I read it, I read both, I bought a subscription to the Astoria paper, thinking or hoping it would be someone else, but I knew it wasn't, and then I guessed it was you writing those emails. The more I thought about it. No one else would have access to the account, and even if they did, they couldn't have done as good a job of impersonating him. You did a really good job."

"Yes, well," Sandra said. "I'm sorry. I really am. Very sorry."

"It's going to be hard for me to remember what was him and what was you. I am already getting them mixed up."

"There's this thing in the literature of grief," Sandra said. "People do things they never would. I didn't believe it at first. And I'm not making excuses. I'm just saying, well I guess I'm trying to tell you I don't know myself. I still don't."

Ryan Whitehurst nodded and smoothed her hands over her jeans.

"The emails aren't even the worst part," Sandra went on. "The worst is you didn't have to lose him. Not the way I did."

"No, not the way you did. But I still would have lost him."

Carl came out and saw where they were and waved and went back inside the house.

"I thought you were shooting today. At the Fillmore."

"There was some hiccup with the insurance, and that messed up the location agreement, so we had to push. Now I think we just won't go there."

"You don't have to be back?"

"No. Not right now."

"Follow me then," Sandra said. "I want to show you something."

She got in her car and backed out and waited for the rental to appear in her rearview. The drive was short, though she had to go some blocks up the hill before finding two parking spots together. They used the side entrance, the wind blowing some cards off a table. Notices for a wedding that had occurred yesterday. When Ryan Whitehurst opened the thick inner door, they saw the sanctuary was mostly empty. A wreath of white flowers stood over the pulpit, and a few members of the choir were unzipping their robes and folding up music stands and carrying them to a locker behind the organ. Two children ran in and chased each other around the carpeted stairs and out again.

Sandra looked at the portrait of stained glass that had puzzled her during the funeral, the man in the suit coat and pince-nez.

A sign with a down arrow directed them to the memorial chapel, and they walked down a ramp and below the pillars that formed an archway over the entrance. Sandra went first. She did not know where to look, if the deceased were arranged by name or date of their death, but Dale's plaque was easy to find since the brass gave off a sheen. In the corners she could make out their reflection.

After reading the inscription Sandra sat on the bench that stood against the wall.

"Dale Francis Tobin," read Ryan Whitehurst. "Them also which sleep in Jesus will God bring with him."

"It's Thessalonians," she added after a moment, scrolling down on her phone.

"Dale's mom was a Bible lover," Sandra said. "I'm not sure if you knew that. She didn't want him cremated."

Ryan Whitehurst stepped closer to the plaque.

"You said in one of the emails it was over right away?"

"As far as we know," said Sandra. "I don't think he ever—you know. I don't think he ever felt anything."

Ryan Whitehurst nodded.

"Here, you take a minute," Sandra said. "This is annoying, to have these last moments with somebody around."

She walked up the low passageway that led back to the sanctuary and past the pews and out the door. As she pulled down the street, she glanced one more time at the doors of the church. Ryan Whitehurst was nowhere to be seen.

Until that morning Sandra had forgotten about Comstock's book. Or prophecy, as she now regarded it. She would have to go back and hunt down the interview, read up on the case studies. Yet already she knew it was the only explanation that fit. For the emails. Her design had gotten away from her, and what started as an act of impersonation, or conjuring, bringing Dale back from the dead, had become something else. One more instance of what she thought could only happen to other people happening to her. She had fallen under the spell.

When she got home, no one was there. Carl's truck was gone. She washed the mug and put the cushions back on the couch and loaded the boxes, two containing Dale's stuff and two with her clothes and books and papers.

She sent a text to Beth and told her she was going to leave the spare key under the loose corner at the top of the back stairs.

Earlier in the week her aunt had sent a package, and Sandra stuffed its contents, the dried fruit and teabags, into the trash, saving the box and bed of bubble wrap. She slid it under the passenger seat and was hoping for a quick ride, yet as she drove down the hill in the direction of the harbor, she saw that one lane of the bridge was closed. Three streams of traffic had to merge into one. It was going to take ten minutes to get across. This was the first time she would attempt the crossing, and she had still not made up her mind whether to look and had only the vaguest sense of where the collision occurred anyway. In the hospital one of the policemen had referred to a bridge truss by number, but when she looked at the poles and stanchions, she couldn't see any numerals.

On the dump truck in front of her the words STAY BACK 200 FEET were painted across the gate, and she decided to focus on that, a glare causing her only once to look down, where a tanker was hauling cars or solar panels, birds riding the gusts in between.

She did not look away from the truck again until passing under the sign that said Washington right lane. Highway 101 opened up then, with fields running to the low hills in the east. Passing through Chinook she saw a fishing trawler motor out of a boathouse, its wake nudging a sailboat that was tethered to a buoy. On the dock a man in tall rubber boots and suspenders was emptying a bucket, the water as it hurled through the air a sudden ripple of light, like a sparkler being thrown.

In Ilwaco she turned off the highway and drove down one of the streets until she was at the turn to Anderson's house. It would not be right, she thought, to leave and not say goodbye, but the lights were off in his house and his truck was not under the shed.

At Cape Disappointment the ranger huts were empty. She wondered if there was some other location where she was supposed to pay admission. She crept slowly through the stalls, scanning the glass to be make sure no one was inside.

The road entered a forest, the evergreens matted down on the windward side, the other trees strung with a hard-fisted fruit she could not identify. At the base of the hill was a clearing, the water on her left hidden by a cloud of mist. She knew now where she was. There were cars in the lot, but she did not see anyone and wrapped the urn in her coat. She climbed the path that led through the dunes, past a fence that was knocked down, most of its slats buried. On the beach seaweed was balled, knotted into streamers, and she saw a fish skeleton propped on one of the rocks in the fire pit, scaly rinds peeling off the web of bone. In the tide wash a cardboard drum lapped in and out, crabs spilling out of one end.

The first time she had ever been here was with Dale, when they stopped on their way out of town, not needing to be at the airport until midnight, for the plane back to Kennedy. They almost turned around after feeling the wind, but Dale said the jetty would give cover, and they crossed the beach, past a man putting lines in the water and a child who was making castles, scooping sand into a bucket with plastic walls and turrets.

They sat against the wall, eating the bread they had bought that morning at one of the bakeries on Exchange Street and talking about Mel and the artifacts in his office. Also how lovely the town of Astoria was, with the view of the channel, and all the old houses and their wraparound porches arrayed along the hillside.

A nice place to live, she might have said, to test his decision and see if he was wavering. How different from New York.

"Want to come with?"

He had asked that at the party, when he invited her on the trip to Oregon. Now he said it again, and when he added, "It's okay, you don't have to tell me now," she knew what her answer would be.

Then he stood up, looked around, and took off his shirt.

"What are you doing?"

"What does it look like," he said, moving his hand over his fly and nodding at the water.

"You know it's like twenty degrees in there," she said.

Wading out in his boxers, he mimed an exaggeration of shivering and dove in. He was under for no more than a minute, and she remembered that while she had seen him naked it was still a shock to see his body out in the open like this, amid all that surf and the roaring in the crags. So fragile, his shoulders and waist, and pale, like something spit from its shell, not meant to be seen.

She set the urn down and took off her shoes and laid them against a log. The beach was coarse, flecked with shells and pellets of stone like shaved ice, and while she could hear the breakers crashing beyond the edge of the jetty, the pool in front of her was clear and shallow, dimpled with little whirlpools that seemed to spin off in front of her when she stepped.

The water made her feet and ankles sore, it was so cold. But she kept going. Twenty, thirty feet out, the depth not changing, the sand smooth and pleated like a washboard.

The urn was sealed with a clasp, the initials of the funeral parlor carved across the bottom. She thumbed the latch open and untwisted the knot of cellophane and tipped the canister forward. This is Dale's body, she thought, the same as I saw on the beach all those years ago, rosy and flushed from the cold. The last of him.

She recited all of these things and more. Still the act did not seem real to her.

The ashes colored the water like a burst of squid ink. Then they were gone, vanished in the ocean's solution.

She put two fingers to her lips and held them there. A long kiss.

There were people standing on the cliffs, she noticed that, and wondered if the ceremony had been observed, or if this next part would be, as she mounted the wall of the jetty and slipped the urn beneath a gap in the stones. She could see shells inside, a soda bottle filled with sand, and hoped the urn was above the water line, out of reach of the highest tide.

She stayed the first night in a motel outside Yakima. She did not want to drive far, knowing how tired she was, and after she hit the two hundred–mile mark she chose the first roadside inn advertising a vacancy. The room had wood paneling on the walls, wire hangers dangling from a rod near the sink. It had not been occupied for some time, judging from the fact that the thermostat was off.

Early the next day she started again, and though her plan had been to get home quickly, in a day or two, she began making stops at scenic overlooks, little towns and byways, anything she saw a sign for, even a prairie dog farm just come open for the season. There was a colt stamping in a ring next to the parking lot, pellets of feed for sale in a gum dispenser.

Up into higher elevations, then, reading the doggerel, the nursery rhymes, that were on the highway now. Click it or ticket. Leave unread, don't be dead.

She drove another hundred miles after nightfall and slept at a rest station outside Missoula. The next day she detoured to Virginia City and wandered through the old hotel and blacksmith shop, went out onto the balcony of the opera house. In the afternoon she stopped at a market, a tent village that in the summer no doubt did a lot of business but was mostly deserted today. There were a few people milling about, day trippers, though from where she could not fathom. And students, a few dozen, possibly on spring break. Some of the tents that were closed had sheets on the flap that showed jewelry for sale and an email address where orders might be placed. Only at the end did she find a few that were open. Strawberries and mesclun were for sale in one, ginseng, jars of preserves, and medicinal creams in the next.

At the end a man in a tasseled leather vest was hawking wood engravings and sculptures. She stepped into the tent, struck by an object that was hanging in the corner. A web of roots jointed with bone, with feathers and other shapes burned into the conch, little knobs and turquoise stones fastened to the tip.

She looked at it a long time before realizing what it was. Not a window ornament or chime. A dream catcher. There were others for sale, smaller ones, some attached to a bottle opener or rabbit's foot. They were scattered in a box, and the card in front explained its provenance, the meaning or purpose of some features, but she didn't read it, thinking already it was kitschy, a sucker purchase. Yet perfect for Tina.

"Ten dollars?" she said, surprised at the sum written on the tag. She was expecting it to be more and handed the money over before he could answer.

At dinner she called Carl. "I saw her yesterday," he said. "They have a policy to stay away at the beginning, for a day or two, but I knew she would want to see Tina."

"And she did, right?"

"Lee? Yeah, she did. Kind of sheepish about the whole thing, though. Embarrassed."

"I can understand that," Sandra said.

"Also, I talked to your detective. He came by the house. I told him we were straight."

"Thank you," Sandra said.

"It's a nice place you found. I wouldn't mind holing up there for a day or two. I mean, not, but you know."

Sandra asked to speak to Tina, and when she came on the line she said, "Sammy, where are you?"

"A good question. I don't really know. In the middle of Montana. Twenty miles to Glendive. That's the last sign I saw."

"Glendive?"

"It's a town, sweetheart. But I'll tell you, I got you something."

"You did? What?"

"Something to hang over your bed. I'm going to mail it to you, to your dad, and you'll get it in a few days."

"Okay."

"How's your mommy? You saw her?"

"Yesterday."

"What was she doing?"

"She had class. She's in school."

"She is?"

"Yeah, she said she's going to make sure it's safe for me. To go to school."

So they hadn't told her after all. But it was okay, Sandra decided. It could wait. Knowledge could wait.

She was on the road for another hour and was pulled over for speeding. She had just come off an on-ramp when the cruiser flashed its lights. She wasn't going more than five miles over the limit and suspected it was an excuse to inspect the car, crammed as it was with boxes and the rug pressed up against the windshield.

The officer wrote a warning and gave it to her, his handwriting lost on the pink carbon. As she was putting away her insurance card and registration she found the key ring, and tried to guess when Ryan Whitehurst would have had the chance to put it in the glove box, a place where Sandra would not immediately see it.

"Is it an heirloom?" she had written, and that was the giveaway, or should have been, though Ryan Whitehurst said she believed Dale simply did not remember the night the way she thought she had. And perhaps that was true. Maybe it did not seem special to him, not at first. Only later, and after a second meeting, would the night assume some significance, take on a new dimension. He would be emailing her, or see her at a screening, and it would be there suddenly, like a visitation, the cantina, playing pool and waiting for the shuttle, full of something he couldn't explain, that he had missed the first time around. And would have to go back for.

But that did not mean—did not necessarily mean—what Sandra had feared, that it was his desire to upend everything, pull up stakes, get a divorce. All it meant was that the affair, like everything else in his life, was unfinished. There hadn't even been time, as it turned out, to determine if it was that or not. An affair.

She brought the key ring into the hotel with her that night and put it in one of the envelopes on the desk. Then she began composing a letter on hotel stationery.

> Dear Ryan,
>
> Thank you for the gift though I am not sure it is mine to keep. If you ever want it back, that's fine, you only have to say the word and I will send it back.
>
> The drive has been fine so far, though I feel like the scout or advance team on a film. There are all these towns with Wild West or national park themes, and driving through them, at this time of year, feels like driving across an empty movie set. Everything is here, ready and assembled, the saloons and corrals, the troughs where the horses are to be watered, yet the cast and crew have yet to arrive.

That was all. In the morning she put the letter in the box with Dale's wallet. It would be better to finish at home. There was more to say. Ryan Whitehurst would want to know what was going on with Tina, and Lee, and Sandra could tell her about other things, about the scholarship set up in Dale's name, for instance.

She could say all this in an email, of course, but a letter would be more sincere, and more evocative of a fresh start.

And then it would be up to Ryan Whitehurst, and she could answer or not answer, yet both outcomes, Sandra decided, would be the right one. Time—the remembering—would make it so. Months from now, when no reply had come and she conceded it never would, she would say no, of course I don't blame her, how could I, not after what I did.

Or—the other version—that's how we became friends. First we were enemies. Such a strange story, she might go on, it makes you think of the fates, characters of the sort you encounter in mythology, two women with the same lover, each having erred or sinned, and trapped now in the constellations.

Later that day, coming out of the eastern flank of Montana, she was caught in a snowstorm. Her lights had been on since noon, with the occasional wisp batting against the windshield, and soon traffic narrowed to a single lane and the thin column of asphalt disappeared. She saw the brake lights of the van when it was no more than a few feet in front of her and slid off to the shoulder.

It was close to a whiteout. She could not see farther than one or two cars ahead, and the other side of the interstate had closed as well. In the glare of a semi's high beams she saw the flurries kicking up like confetti, and the trees on the edge of the road were sagging. There was an alert on her phone, a blizzard warning with several counties named, though she did not know the one she was in at present. She turned off the ignition to conserve what fuel was left, but worried about the battery failing, so she put the key back in and turned the engine on. A gray and washy light filled the car and she put her head back on the hood of her parka.

The smell of exhaust woke her, and she noticed people getting out of their cars, wandering down the far slope to go to the bathroom. A few sat on lawn chairs. One person in ski goggles, sipping from a koozie.

A tap on the window startled her. She pressed to lower the glass, but it was frozen, and when she opened the door she had to duck to avoid a shower of snow. She covered Tina's dream catcher and saw the face of an older man, the hairs of his beard tipped with ice.

"You all by yourself?" he said.

The snow on the hood was piled high, over the wipers, and it was blowing through the trees in thick, gauzy curtains.

"Why is the road closed?" she asked, for she had been imagining an accident like Dale's, a tractor trailer jackknifing, taking a car out with it. "Is it just the snow," she said, "or something else?"

“Just the snow. But I got a buddy up there with a CB,” he said, pointing into the distance, “and he says it’s not going to be too much longer.”

“Like ten minutes not much longer or two hours?”

He raised his hands to say he didn’t know. She thanked him and watched as he strolled to the car behind, to deliver the same news.

She wondered if the snow had gathered around her tires and downshifted to reverse. The car did not move. She was going to have to clear it away.

Wait. She could hear Dale saying that. Wait until it stops. There’s no sense in doing it before then.

But there won’t be time, she wanted to say. This isn’t our house, we’re not talking about the porch walk. The plows will be by soon, with their blinking yellow strobes, churning out salt and sand. The road would open. There was nothing in the car, though. Nothing she had packed. She would have to use her hands, kneel down in the drifts. And she could do that. Any minute now she would. Shovel herself out.